# "Desecration"

First published June 2021

## Opening verses of The Valley of the Dragon

Roger Turner
Poet

*'Deep in the past*
*in legends and lore*
*Dragons were plenty*
*yet, we see them no more*

*Dragons were awful*
*that's what we're told*
*they killed and left waste*
*and they all loved their gold'*

DESECRATION
ROBBIE COTTRELL

Meet the author
Robert (Robbie) Cottrell

With special thanks to Ian Nicholson, Toni Mount, Rosalind Juma, Raymond Hudson and the members of the Gravesend Writing Group

PARKINSON'S UK
CHANGE ATTITUDES.
FIND A CURE.
JOIN US.

With thanks to the staff at King's College Hospital, Denmark Hill, London

Other books by Robbie Cottrell

Factual books

Thomas Doggett Coat & Badge
(300 years plus of history)

The Badge (the truth)

******

Fictional books

Mister Doggett
The Tide Waiter
The Arsonist
The Clergyman
The Flag
A Pinch of Salt
The Forgotten King
The Ghost of the Ninth
Pestilence and Fire
The Scapegoat
The Man from Huntingdon
The Greatness of Kings
The Custodians of Time
Trials and Tribulations

******

Ian Nicholson (author and editor)
Toni Mount (author and mentor)

Rosalind Juma

Rosalind Juma is a highly respected and talented poet, who has already embellished my books with her magical poetic works - I bid you welcome to another entitled

*"Thy servant Alcuin"*

Stories that claim to be ‘based on a true story’ mix fact with fiction by taking events that happened in real life but alter certain details, this differs from historical fiction. In historical fiction the plot is original, but the settings and/or characters are based on real life.

This book does not reflect the author's opinions but is based on those revealed from contemporary sources.

MISTER DOGGETT

THE
TIDEWAITER

THE
ARSONIST
ROBBIE COTTRELL

THE CLERGYMAN
A MAN OF PURE EVIL
FEATURING
JOHN CRAWFORD
BY
ROBBIE COTTRELL

THE FLAG
BY
ROBBIE COTTRELL

A pinch of salt
by
Robbie Cottrell
(author of "THE FLAG")

The
Forgotten King

Robbie Cottrell

The Greatness
Of
Kings'

Thomas Doggett's Coat and Badge
The oldest annual sporting event held in the world
A report on every race since 1715

Rob returns to his roots by examining the varying inaccuracies and fanciful tales told of Doggett's Coat and Badge.

From the pages of Wikipedia

*Desecration is the act of depriving something of its sacred character, or the disrespectful, contemptuous, or destructive treatment of that which is held to be sacred or holy by a group or individual.*

*Many consider acts of desecration to be sacrilegious acts. This can include desecration of sacred books, sacred places or sacred objects.*

## ***Thy servant Alcuin***

*Mine esteemed bishop, Higbald, I wish I never knew*
*How the skywards portent of dragon shapes*
*Came to be our Holy Island slew*
*Monks of Holy Order slaughtered*
*Christ's manuscripts destroyed*
*No mercy, nor of reverence*
*Of sword wielding Viking men deployed*
*These marauders knew not what they killed*
*More than shed blood of monastic men*
*Can heathens comprehend gospels sent from our almighty?*
*Embossed with gold through pen?*
*Can their ignorance defend them?*
*Still, warring is ill conceived destroyer*
*Motive to take what is not yours*
*Makes evil your employer*
*I ponder, in my prayer times*
*Didst divine vengeance fall on this fair-isle*
*Through accommodating Sicga's body to rest*
*Guilty of regicide and suicide, he*
*Conspired to kill Northumbrian King*
*Then conscience could not withstand the test*
*Ignoble deeds, dastardly thoughts*
*Which dwelt within his being*
*Should not receive reward of holy resort*
*As the Almighty all is seeing*
*I grieve for our Holy, pillaged Island*
*Sorrow for the Sanctus' way of being*
*My prayer, from Charlemagne, prayed from the heart*
*Be that mercy from our Lord May impart*
*Changed fortune for our Holy Isle*
*May light and healing raise a smile*
*Within our first enshrined Christian community*
*May faith and valour there thrive*
*With graced impunity.*

# CHAPTER ONE

*"A boatless man is tied to the land."*

From the Hávamál or the Sayings of Odin

Before beginning my saga, I must first tell you I have always been more of an intellectual than a warrior which is highly unusual for a Dane; but most of which I will tell you is bizarre, even for a Viking.

My name is Ragnar Thorgilssen. My father, the Jarl, named me Ragnar after one our greatest warrior Ragnar Lothbrok; although my father never knew or met with him, every Dane knew of him and his exploits. Lothbrok was the best fighter ever to come from the lands in the north. Ragnar was born and raised near the Kattegat Sea in Daneland or Normanni, which meant - *"men from the north"*

My passion for knowledge, understanding and learning has forever been persistent, certainly since my childhood days. By the time I reached puberty if anyone brought forth a map and set it before me, I could immediately put forward, by checking the terrain and the surrounding countryside, which army was likely to gain a glorious victory, and which would probably lick their wounds after suffering a bloody sickening defeat; my predictions were seldom incorrect. My brothers only believed in rushing blindly forward, charging with sword in hand, kill and rout the opposing force; thus leaving plenty of time to get drunk and hump as many maidens they could lay their hands on.

About this time, when I was old enough to hold a sword my grandfather, Knudsen, gave me sound advice which I promised him never to forget.

He explained that those who drank to excess were lesser beings than the squirrels of the woods, his exact words being - *'most animals after feeling the effects of drink would never again think of drinking from the same source again, thereby making squirrels much wiser than most men.'*

The Jarl, who just happened to be my father, had placed me in command of my own boat, too early for my thinking; thankfully he chose an experienced seaman to be my steersman and nautical advisor.

Due to my physical weaknesses the crew eyed me with misgivings. I seldom socialised or drank with them, and as for being in the front rank of a shield wall with them, you can forget it, all that shouting and cursing gave me headaches.

I was forever reminding father, *'I was the thinker and not a fighter,'* to which he normally replied that one day he would have need of me, but what that need was to be he never revealed, although I hoped that by succeeding in this, my virgin voyage, he might, at least, reveal his plans for me.

I detested the thought of keeping secrets from my friend and tutor Redwald, but as I was unaware of the Jarl's plan, I could hardly call them a secret.

There was another entity which I have to explain, although it is more of an annoyance to me and certainly not a secret to those around me; my stomach had always been intolerant to the excesses of mead, and on the rare occasion when I felt obliged to participate in a prolonged drinking session either to celebrate an impressive victory or father's birthing date, I would be forced to hide away in my own quarters to vomit and gag for days on end.

I was the rarest kind of Viking - unable to drink and too weak to make any difference in the shieldwall, even the shieldmaidens teased me by trying to grab my cock while pretending to castrate me with their seaux; the girls thought it would be fun by insinuating my utter uselessness as a warrior.

I was my father's youngest son with characteristics unlike any of my siblings; I was tall and slender of build, while my brothers were as wide as they were tall; they were constantly getting into scraps while I read inside my father's great hall; my brothers drank to excess, making fools of themselves, an activity I always shied away from. Mother had always said I was the prettiest of a bad bunch, I had sun-bleached fair hair which I tied together on the crown of my head; there had always been rumours that I was conceived when father was away, if this was true or not my father always treated me exactly the same as my kin-folk; my eyes were deep blue just like my mother's, unlike the rest of father's brood all of whom had hazel coloured eyes. I never seeked father's favour, you will therefore understand my amazement when he selected me to choose a crew for a special voyage, naturally the first man on my crew list was my uncle and guardian - Redwald; the rest of the crew I left in the capable hands of Uncle Redwald.

I knew I could never expect to make a name for myself as a warrior, but as a mapmaker, that was where my future lay, and where I was happiest.

One last matter, I must confess that I had always endured the cruellest kind of motion sickness, predominately when sailing. The sea-gods had cursed me since birth with this affliction or it might be that Loki, the trickster god, was punishing me by presenting me with a gift that I never wanted - a horrendous sea-belly, I suppose that was the kind of trick Loki would play.

Tactics, wisdom and knowledge were considered to be my strong points; when any of my four brothers returned from raiding the lands to our south I sought out any scrolls or books they returned with; although my brothers never could understand the written words, they just loved the pretty coloured pictures within the books, especially those depicting naked men and women; the scrolls and parchments normally were used to wipe their arses on.

Uncle Redwald had often told me that whilst strength was imperative in a warrior, we should never forget the importance of intelligence and strategy, *or,* as he expressed it - *'know your enemy, do as they do, but do it quicker.'*

Redwald was a close friend of my parents, they were unrelated, but custom dictated I should call him uncle. He was only a few years older than me, but he was a brute of man, tall in stature and slightly overweight, but I dared not tell him he was fat in his face. He had fought in many encounters and he carried the scares of a few of them across his face. One such scare prevented him from growing a full-beard as his left cheek had been sliced open to the jawbone; it made him look fiercer than he actually was. He was proud of his wounds and took every opportunity of showing them to the village children. Uncle Redwald had never married, although I knew for a fact he had at least three children living in the surrounding villages.

Uncle Redwald was thought to have pathways inside his head that enabled him to talk to the spirits of those who had gone before us; he even conversed with the gods.

Being the youngest son of the Jarl it was my duty, as well as my responsibility to calculate the purchasing of supplies as well as estimating the time we spent at sea, as well as making sure my sneekja was sea worthy and fully prepared for every eventuality.

The *'Sea Slicer',* for that is the name of my longboat, was to be ready for sailing in the night of the first full moon following the slaughter month, or as we called it the first month after Yuletime known Gormánaðar

To gain access to the open sea from Aarhus it was my intention to sail east before swinging northward until we sighted the small village of Frederickshavn on our port bow, this is where I intended to haul down our sail and have the crew row those final leagues before anchoring within the safe confines of Albaek Bay, to make sure our hull had no leaks requiring attention.

I always wondered why men always called their vessels female; my father had once told me it was because they were cows to handle until you got used to their outlandish behaviour; but if treat them with respect they will love you for all eternity and forever obey you. I never knew if this was his joke nor was he truthful.

Throughout the decades, its natural harbour was close to the northern edge of the bay and enjoyed a protected, safe anchorage, but the high mountain streams that incessantly flowed into the fjord from the snowy peaks fed the great fjord with sandy stone silt. As the streams slowed they gradually narrowed, leaving us worried that the great fjord would become so congested with silt and mud even our shallowest barges would be unnavigable beyond the fringes of the fjord, unless the moon was at its fullest, signifying the importance on the spring tides.

After departing Albaek Bay my intention was to sail east until the coastline of home gradually faded from view, then under full we would navigate true north until we reached the open sea and thereon to the great Northern Ocean.

Legend has it, that King Dan gave his name to every Dane; Great King Dan was the son of the mighty Hun Humblus, both being known as warriors of immense strength and enormity.

We Danes had heard rumours regarding the Anglo-Saxons; it appeared they had displeased the old gods by converting to a strange religion where the god they worshipped had apparently died on a wooden cross somewhere towards the eastern end of, what was called the Middle Sea, which we now call the Mediterranean.

My father, was a man known for his riddles and brain teasers; he once told me that - *'the strongest will not be those who survive, and those without intelligence will also fail to survive.'*

I waited in anticipation for him to complete his riddle, but he strangely kept silent until he became fully aware of my impatience.

*'Who will survive if not the strongest or the most gifted amongst us?'* I asked, trying not to show my irritation.

My father, Jarl Tor Thorgilssen, smiled before answering me with these words; - *'It is the man who is the most adaptable to change, it is he who will survive.'*

It made sense to me and I promised my father to always remember those wise words.

I still failed to understand why my father had chosen me to lead this current mission; I even told him surely one of my brothers would have been better qualified. His reply was brief and to the point - *'if I wanted this mission to fail I would have sent one of your brothers, but as I want it to succeed I chose you.'*

With my father's words echoing inside my head I walked aft and sat beside Redwald on the steering bench and reflected on what might lay ahead, but for whatever reason I could not look at my uncle and steersman in the eye, as he might have recognised the private agony I was deliberately holding back inside my stomach, if the waters proved angry my breakfast and last night's supper would spill out into the sea.

I had to smile as I considered Loki tricking and misguiding those idiotic Anglo-Saxon usurpers travelling the wrong path towards Christianity; such misgivings and falsehoods would prove their eventual ruination. I silently prayed to Loki that he might offer to take away the curse of my sea-belly.

Redwald noticed the smile on my face as he looked at me in surprise, unaware what he should say, *'if in doubt say nothing,'* he kept the thought to himself.

The Angles, Jutes and Saxons had undeniably angered the old gods in some way, and for whatever reason their armies had to heavily rely on their new mysterious god to keep them protected. I had no reason to solicit Odin or Thor to aid us in our voyage of discovery for the omens all looked positive.

The crew expressed their amusement when Redwald, my steersman, spoke of Loki's trickery and the gods powers of deception, '*we will simply walk ashore and greet those brainless Anglo-Saxons; but instead of offering them the hand of friendship they will taste our deadly seax cutting deep into their flesh.*' Redwald must have been reading my mind as we simultaneously thought of Loki at the same time. Redwald, like my father was full of riddles and quotes, although he told me had made up the puzzles himself, but I think this was untrue, let's just say that Redwald was full of something.

Our expectations were extremely high as we had been chosen by our Jarl to be the first Viking longboat to sail across the vast expanse of the great Northern Ocean to set foot on a land where the soil was allegedly rich with innumerable crops, more than a man could count, where cattle, sheep and pigs could graze all seasons long on the lush green pastures and flowery meadows of the Angel Isle.

The Angles and Saxons were growing fat and lazy on this plentiful green and pleasant land, a land we would take from them by agreement or by force if necessary. We had always dreamed of a future living in Britain where our people visualised and marvelled at the joy the gods were gifting us.

A beautiful and truly fruitful land!

Odin revealed his greatest prophecy to the blood-seers telling them to notify his people that before the next Gormánaðar, we would all, each and every one of us taste the true riches the gluttonous Anglo-Saxons were denying us.

I notified Redwald and the crew that our intended beaching point was on the north-east coast of the dual kingdoms of Norþan-hymbre, known as Bernicia and all the lands north of the Humber and the land of Deira to the south. I had further informed the crew our plotted landfall would be close to the unprotected rocky Christian islet of Lindisfarena, known to the Christians as Holy Island, where it is said significant wealth is hidden. The island was only connected to the mainland by a man made narrow causeway when the water is low; Lindisfarena was known to be a place of healing as well as being one of the holiest Christian sites in all of Britannica. However, all of this was untrue; my father's intention all along, was to sail further south to the Anglo-Saxon stronghold of Waymouthe in Dornsaete. It seemed that he needed to know why the Saxons had purposely built such fortifications in the area.

I was certain Redwald knew of the rouse, for was it not he who advised me to know your enemy, do as they do, but do it quicker!

We had been instructed that our raid on Lindisfarena would shake Christianity to its foundations; but what confused me, assuming we would one day raid the small island was why the Anglo-Saxons had ignored the possibility of any assault coming from the sea. Evidently they knew nothing of the Danes nautical abilities.

The Anglo-Saxon's misguided faith would prove their ultimate downfall; and our raid would prove to be our greatest triumph. It was then that my father's words rang deep inside my head - *'It is the man who is the most adaptable to change who will survive.'*

It is said we Danes had adapted quicker to change, and because of our adaption we had survived, but I wondered if the Anglo-Saxon had adjusted himself to those changes as well as us.

Our sailing from the anchorage within Albaek Bay was forcibly delayed until the afternoon's tide due to a puzzling thick mist that covered the complete surface of the bay. The seers had predicted fine weather all the way to the northern Anglo-Saxon heartlands; our seers were never wrong, so I had to ask myself what was the cause of this perplexing unnatural mist, and what was the cause. It could be a sign from the gods or maybe the trickster Loki was still playing his childish pranks?

The uncanny mist alarmed some of the younger crewmen into thinking it was a bad omen as they looked to me in calming their wavering spirits.

I had others matters to contend with, the weather conditions within the bay were said to be completely tranquil but once we had cleared what should have been the calm waters of the Kattegat Sea; with Skagen point on our port bow I had to steer directly into the path of the unpredictable waters of the Great Northern Ocean.

I had only sailed the ocean once previous with my father, who although he being an experienced seaman, even he, with all his strength of mind and experience found headway hard to achieve.

But first I had to overcome my one fear, or to be precise the one fear neither maps nor tactics could ever control - my sea-belly sickness!

The seers had studied these types of perplexing medical conditions and explained the likely cause of my sickness; I had read various medical books regarding sailing sickness, and it seemed the source of this sickness was caused by erratic and continuous shifting of a vessel whilst underway. It seemed that my brain was detecting unusual movement changes, from up and down and sideways. I knew the voyage would leave me with feelings of exhaustion, nausea and dizziness, but hopefully the sickness would pass all being well, within one day. Sickness might be a reality to some, but not for a son of a Jarl, with a reputation to live up to.

The afternoon tide came and went, but the dense mist lingered, there was no shifting the murkiness that shrouded our anchorage. I could only make out the twinkling oil lamps of Aarhus in the distance but the stench of rotting gutted fish had not left our nostrils. The sole lovers of that beloved reek were the countless gulls circling endlessly overhead.

It quickly became obvious that we would not be leaving our anchorage until tomorrow's tide. I gave permission for half the crew to go ashore as a gesture of goodwill. I presumed this would probably the last time their feet would stand on mother earth until we beached on British soil.

Redwald accompanied the men to make sure they didn't get out of hand, or bother the townsfolk. Meanwhile I arranged a bed for me in the prow, for this might be my last uninterrupted sleep until we arrived in northern Britain.

Both tender boats thumped alongside *Sea Slicer's smooth wooden hull* sometime after the moon slide behind a covering of ever blackening cloud, the thump heralded the crew's return. The unnatural fog partially relented, but the murkiness holding us within its grasp held us sufficiently making a safe departure impossible.

Something was wrong; a commotion towards the steering bench brought me from a sound sleep, the turmoil had abruptly ended my wondrous dreams.

*'Is that women I hear.'* that was all I remembered until I tried to lifting my head from my sheepskin pillow the following morning. As I gazed out from my bleary eyes the sun was already bright in the sky, but what was significant is that the sky was bright blue - the fog had lifted, but my head dejectedly declined - *'Føkka,'*

# CHAPTER TWO

*"Drunk I was, I was over-drunk,*
*at that cunning Fjalar's.*
*It's the best drunkenness,*
*when every one after it regains his reason."*

From the Hávamál or the Sayings of Odin

I again tried lifting my head from the pillow to no avail; it simply felt as though an axe had split my head wide open. Not only had I drank too much, my stomach felt it was on fire, a feeling of being burnt from the inside out. While I slept I had accidently vomited over my tunic and leggings; my manhood was exposed for all to see, due to pissing myself.

*'Føkka,'* I cried again, but it was too late, my head ached from the juddering noise inside my head.

I tried one last time to raise my head from the pillow - it was then that the pain hit me, I look about myself peering through half-closed puffy red-eyes; *'where is Redwald,'* I gently enquired. Redwald should be at the steering arm someone replied. Eventually Redwald waddled towards me from his post by the steering arm and sat beside me in my temporary bed within the prow. He showed little sign of sympathy; if I didn't know any better it seemed Redwald was enjoying himself due to my drunken predicament. Speaking as quietly as possible I asked, *'what happened last night?'*

Redwald beamed through his toothless grin as he tried to explain the events of the previous evening; *'you asked for six young maidens to be brought out to the boat and after you humped your way through all of them - you passed out. Afterwards I personally escorted the ladies back to Albaek and offered each one a silver coin for their services.*

*As their fathers were being rather troublesome and noisy I decided to place a piece of hack gold into their dirty grubby palms; although if it was down to me I would have kept the gold and hacked off their fucking fingers, but I must tell you this, if you value your life, it would be best if you never show your handsome little face in Albaek again. Those thieving fathers might forget to recognise you but I doubt if those girls will, especially if they are cuddling a small bundle about their bodies.'*

I tried to take in everything in Redwald had just said, but I remained baffled, *'where did you get the money from?'*

Redwald smiled gave another toothless grin as he turned to toddle away to his steering bench. *'I borrowed it from your pocket while you slept,'* he replied, to which the whole crew cheered.

I hurriedly pulled my leggings about my waist and felt inside my pockets, *'there's nothing there,'* I shouted as my head vibrated to the sound of my own vocal chords.

*'Thought you wouldn't mind if I tipped the lads,'* Redwald shouted back, he was really enjoying my frailty.

I desperately tried to find the correct words to say but my agony was so acute and as yet we remained at the anchorage. I studied the bay for a brief moment, it reminded me of shimmering glass, and there wasn't a single ripple to be seen over its surface, with the absence of any breeze or puff of air I ordered the lads to bring up the anchor and be ready to steadily row us clear from our prison call, for that was how I remembered it, an anchorage that had long held us captive.

*'Við dauði Þórs',* I shouted which roughly translated meant *'by Thor's death.'* Although inside me I considered Loki to be the likely cause for our delay. I was angry with myself and with Loki, not so much for the delay, but for being unable to remember if I had put a smile on any of those six girl's faces. I hope I did honour them, if not my hangover would be a waste of time.

Redwald took one final glance in my direction and shouted, *'Ragnar, you humped them well.'*

Throughout the morning I tried to keep busy, knowing that every set of eyes derided me. I was furious with myself and the only way to satisfy my fury was to take it out on the crew. *'Unhook that dragon head from the prow';* I shouted at two idle looking men, *'we don't want the Saxon's to think we are raiding, we have to try and convince them we are traders.'*

I felt betrayed, angry and furious, but it wasn't the fault of being delayed, as the master of the boat the responsibility of success or failure fell on my shoulders.

I put my right hand into the ice-cool waters of the bay and softly prayed to the god of the sea, Aegir; I promised him great riches if we returned; I told him the crew were hungry for battle against the Anglo-Saxons who no longer sought the old gods for shelter. I lovingly caressed Thor's hammer about my neck as I prayed to Aegir, the sea god for his guidance. My ship was ready to sail but I feared Loki was still playing games with us.

I suddenly realised that my blonde hair was brushing against my eyes, it irritated me until I recognised the meaning - initially it was just a mere breeze drifting across the water, it came out of nowhere in particular, but nevertheless a breeze it was.

Redwald had already felt the light wind on his back and instinctually knew what it meant - *'make sail',* he bellowed. *'Be sharp about you for whatever wind we might have could cease before we clear the bay.'*

The crew jumped about carrying out their duties with relish, they were happy and didn't give them a second thought. They had been well drilled by Uncle Redwald who was like a father figure to them; even though he resembled the powerful white bear that lived further north, we all respected and loved him.

A thought suddenly popped into my head, how many of those on board had Redwald fathered?

With the anchor stowed in the prow our sail quickly filled with the wind and finally *'Sea Slicer'* was doing what she loved best, slicing through the water cutting her way through the waves as effortlessly as a hot knife cuts through cold whale fat.

We swiftly rounded Skagen point and before us lay the volatile open waters of the Great Northern Ocean. *Sea Slicer* was happiest when the waves relentlessly licked at her smooth hull; she reacted like a maiden being humped for the first time; she tasted the glorious salted water like a new born suckling upon her mother's teats. *Sea Slicer* ploughed onwards, offering us the thrill of riding an unbroken horse that continuously thrashed violently in ever decreasing circles as it tried to unseat its rider.

Father was right, boats are similar to women, treat them with respect and they will love you forever and they will always obey and remain faithful to you.

Without thinking I suddenly realised I no longer had the pangs of sickness; could it be there were too many other things going on about me. My brain was hell bent on the tasks that lay ahead. I did worry by the height of the waves as water spilled into our bilge. For a briefest of time I wholly lost sight of the horizon. The cold bitter wind howled steadily from the north increasing our headway.

The crew seemed happy as they sang their songs of victories and desires. Salt water was continually bailed from the bilges; but they went about their duties without a care in the world.

And as we sailed I was proud of them!

At sunset on that first day at sea everything abruptly changed, as I thought it probably would. The darkening skies became illuminated with vivid bolts of lightning accompanied by jagged flashes criss-crossing the night sky. Thor's heavy hammer busily thrashed down on us that night.

We couldn't tell if the flashes of bright sparkling light came from the heavens down or from the sea upward, all we knew was that a wild and ferocious storm had crashed into us and we soon would be right in the middle of the squall. We had little choice but to ride it out; oars were carefully stowed beneath the rowing benches and our canvas sail once hauled in and secured was placed above our heads, but it gave us little protection from the wind that blew with ever increasing ferocity.

All through that night I truly admit to seeing at least three dragons dancing high in the blackened night sky, if it were ever possible what we witnessed that night was a darker gloominess than black; the waves were so high that at one time we lost sight of the horizon for what appeared an eternity. The bitter cold wind continued to howl, as the huge waves continued to batter us; it relentlessly without mercy smashed against the hull like a demon splintering *Sea Slicer's* flimsy timbers, thankfully with the exception of one broken rib and a fractured plank our leaking hull held firm.

Redwald cried out above the noise of the storm, *'looks like Loki and Aegir are fighting for supremacy of the oceans; who knows how many leagues we had been blown off course.'*

Hailstones began crashing down on our heads like pebbles being thrown deliberately on our unprotected bodies. Thunder crashed again and the repeated sounds of explosions blasted our ears just as the rain intensified in its ferocity.

I was not the only one who pissed his pants that night! Fear is likened to a sense of dread and trepidation, it alerts you to the possibility that you can never awake from your nightmares!

We Norsemen had always considered ourselves to best trained seamen in the world; we had sailed where no man had sailed before; there are those who thought if you sailed such distances you would fall off the end of the world; legend has it that one of our longboats sailed past Norðreyjar and continued its voyage to a new world; but nothing could have ever trained us against the fury of the gods on that frightful night as they waged war in the heavens above. The tempest had trapped us, twisting and turning us the gales encircled *'Sea Slicer'* holding us hostage; making it impossible to navigate by the night stars for even the moon and stars had been held captive tonight by the gods. In my ten years of navigation, after being taught how to navigate by the stars, moon and clouds, nothing could have prepared me for what that night held in store. We were held tight in tan explosive thunderstorm, all we could do was sit tight, hang on for dear life and wait until the storm subsided; hopefully I could by then recalculate our position. I suggested two of our heavier men go about the boat to ensure the crew had wrapped a tightened guide rope about their waists which they securely attached around the *Sea Slicer's* ribs.

Redwald sensibly ordered half the crew to continue bailing the bilge whilst the other half slept, and continue in four hours shifts until the imminent danger of being swamped had abated.

Neither Redwald nor I slept that night; we both fell about the longboat encouraging the crew, giving them strength, for we both knew the stories of longboats being swamped by a rogue wave resulting in the total loss of life and cargo.

I had to come to terms that neither Redwald nor I were able to calculate our exact location; without that important piece of the jigsaw we had no way of plotting a course.

My sea-belly started to rumble as I tried albeit unsteadily to stand, I cupped my hands about my mouth and shouted in fury to Loki *'Streð Mik.'* But I don't think he hear, as my bile flowed again from my mouth and I started to wretch.

We felt trapped, a feeling not dissimilar to a cork bobbing up and down on the water as 'Sea Slicer' continued her drifting on her unknown course.

I thanked the gods that our Danish boat builders were the best in the world. If we had sailed in an Anglo-Saxon vessel we would be at the bottom of the sea by now, drowned and forgotten; easy fodder for the sea monsters that live in the lower regions of the Great Northern Ocean. Once again bile flowed from my lips at the thought of monsters from the deep sucking the meat from our bones.

Our craftsmen had long learned the skill of constructing our longboats by cladding the hull in a clinker formation where every plank runs forward to aft each plank overlapping the next.

Clinker built, is also known as lapstrake, and has always been our preferred method of boat building, a hull where the edges of each plank overlaps the next.

Where necessary in larger vessels, shorter planks could be joined end to end to form a longer strake or hull plank.

The Anglo-Saxons have always relied on constructing their various craft by means of carvel planking, a method of boat building whereby every plank is laid edge on edge, fastened to a robust frame, to form one smooth surface. The gap between each plank is later caulked with a mixture of wool and pitch.

We all prayed to the gods that night to keep us safe until morning came, that is if we were all alive come morning.

# CHAPTER THREE

*"The more attention you pay to your surroundings,*
*the safer you are going to be.*
*I see smoke, smoke means fire, fire means people,*
*people means we should get out quickly."*

From the Volsunga Saga

Redwald was first to wake, his movements brought me out of an uneasy sleep; I fully expected *Sea Slicer* to be washed ashore on some foreign soil; but to my utter amazement we had survived everything the storm had thrown at us. Redwald grabbed hold of my left arm to assist my rising, the fingers of my right hand gripped tightly around Thor's hammer.

I stretched my body to its fullest height and joined him in fixing our eyes on a truly magnificent site; as a beautiful glowing circle had miraculously ascended from the depths of the ocean bed to reveal itself in all its glory and splendour. The sun's dazzling light transformed the dreary early morning sky into a spectacular array of colours.

A distant rainbow firmly illustrated god's power by changing his fiercesome war-bow into the tranquillity of our peaceful ambitions. The purpose of our voyage was to seek nothing except peace and harmony between Viking and Anglo-Saxon, however if that peace was achievable, or not, we had to wait and see and be patient. The giant ball of fire gradually reached further towards the heavens, and as it did numerous sunbeams pierced all it surveyed as it seeked out the remnants of the darkness. The sun's strength and heat was that intense we had to shield our eyes to prevent the risk of catching sun blindness.

Sunrise is truly a beautiful site to those who truly took the time to gaze at the scene.

The gods had listen to my prayers last night and granted us life.

As we continued to observe the unravelling spectacle we found the surrounding waters took on renewed vibrant colours; the ocean utterly seized us in its grasp, both of us were captivated, unable to turn our eyes the magnificence it beheld. It is truly amazing how effortlessly the sun can put on a show and display such a scene as a sunrise can have on the spirit. The surface of water continued to dazzle us. We watched in awe as the unblemished purity of colours fashioned by the sun's rays enabled the dawning of a new day to take on radiance like no other; the sun god, Sol, had created such morning as the sign of renewal of life. I had never before witnessed so many changes in the colour within the sky that reflected upon the waters, from turquoise to azure to aqua and back again to a celestial blue. We had been distracted by the continuous changing of colours that for a moment we had forgotten the sun as it climbed higher and higher into the morning sky.

A morning we thought never again to see!

The crew had been hard at work throughout the night and it was thanks to their e, coupled with Sol's approval to offer us life that we survived the terrors of the night, but I wondered what horrors might await us throughout the day.

We had other matters to contend with as most of our rations had not been as successful, most were at the bottom of the sea and some of which remained had been contaminated. However we resorted to what we Danes normally do in time of crisis - the waters being plentiful with fish, we sailors lowered hook and line into the water and helped ourselves to the gods gracious bounties, although I much preferred eating fish hot as opposed to eating it raw but beggars can never be choosers.

In an attempt to lift the crew's morale I suggested Redwald should speak regarding the Danes formidable and fearsome reputation throughout adversaries.

Redwald sat on his beloved steering bench, cleared his throat and wiped the remains of any fish scales from his beard; his face glowed with emotion as he began -

*'We Danes will forever sail from our homeland to raid whatever and whoever we want throughout the southern mainland and its islands. Our attacks have always been cleverly planned, daring and give no warning; this way our victories seldom fade from our enemy's hearts. In Viking society, honour and glory in battle and being unafraid in combat, for we have been promised a place within the great halls of Valhalla, where Odin himself greets us with open arms. For it has been foretold, since the beginning of time, we will meet again with our friends to drink, eat, laugh and brawl. We Danes are not like the Romans who left our lands with their tail between their legs; we will, without question, follow our chieftain and their sons into the darkness of hell,'* at the mention of the word son Redwald turned and placed his arm about my shoulders in a sincere act of brotherhood.

*'The Saxons fear us and call us pirate raiders, so let us this day welcome the sun and pray to Odin for his bounteous rewards.'*

Redwald finished his rousing speech and sat comfortably on his wet steering bench grabbing hold of the steering arm, to the rapturous sound of cheering.

My friend was truly a remarkable warrior, he touched every extremity of aggressiveness to that of humiliation, in that morning I had seen both.

We welcomed the coming of the morning sun as it pierced the darkness of the outrageous events we had endured throughout the night. The morning felt fresh and still, no longer did we fear the ocean's mêlée. We watched the large lustrous ball continued to rise and grow in stature from the calmness of the distant horizon; bring warmth to the obscured morning sky. The life giving orb cast its sunbeams in every direction it touched while it continued illuminating all within its circle. We stared in wonderment by the transformation it gradually fashioned with the passing time.

The morning sky was a joy to behold; the sun radiated its strength as it gradually climbed higher and higher in the fullness of the heavens above.

The moon lingered briefly in the western sky before slowly descending into the depths of the open arms of the waiting ocean before settling quietly beneath the watery horizon. All of us witnessed an epic closing night best forgotten. *'Let us greet the rebirth of the bright, life giving sun,'* I reverently praised the gods for their protection during the night.

Perhaps I had been too hasty in placing the blame on Thor and Aegir for creating such turmoil within the blackened skies. I recalled my bloodfather's foretelling of two minor gods - Sól and Máni. Might these two demi-gods be responsible for the churning of the ocean, and the destruction it caused within the darkened sky, and those deadly thunderbolts caused hailstones to be thrown upon our unprotected heads?

My 'bloodfather maintained, albeit with dread and trepidation, that the gods were untouchable; in Norse culture each and every one of us must live in fear of the wrath of gods.

*'According to the seers knowledge, Sól the sun goddess drove her chariot to the sun, across the day time sky,'* I pointed to the sun so that Redwald followed my lesson. *'Her brother Máni chased his sister, by taking a duplicate journey which represented the moon. Sól and Máni never journeyed alone; Sól was forever being pursued by a ferocious wolf named Hati; while her brother Máni was constantly in fear of his life by Hati's sister, the she-wolf named Sköll.'*

I could tell that Redwald was intoxicated with the tale, especially that incessant chase Sól and Máni found themselves.

*'Did they ever find relief to find happiness,'* Redwald, the strongest, fiercest and yet humblest sailor in the longboat, was uncontrollable as he wept whilst I answered his question.

*'The bloodfather's told us that one day Sól and Máni will stand their ground and confront the evil Hati and Sköll and a great battle in the sky will ensue leading*

*to the death of a vast number of great figures, natural disasters and the submersion of the world in water will follow. After this truly deadly encounter the world will resurface anew and become fertile; those that remain will join with the returning gods and the world will eventually be repopulated by the seed of two human survivors.'*

Redwald looked confused for he recalled the tales he had heard from the enslaved Christian monks who told of a similar tale. He shook his head and turned back to his seat by his beloved steering bench.

*'Redwald,'* I shouted, *'Ragnarök is the place in our mythology where it has been foretold that a great battle to end all battles will take place. Every Germanic tribe is aware of the truth of Ragnarök together with Odin's foretelling, and that including* the Jutes and the Anglo-*Saxons.'*

*'We Vikings know of the whereabouts of Valhalla and Ragnarök, but I very much doubt if the Christians or their dead god know of Ragnarök or its significance.'*

Redwald looked weary as he replied, for he had been witness to many a battle to last a full lifetime, *'Odin will demanded that only his most courageous and fearsome fighters should join him on the battlefield of Ragnarök. You have no foretelling of when these events at Valhalla and Ragnarök will come to pass, together with the ultimate apocalyptic finale within our legends and traditions; but when that battle begins, rest assured our enemies will be the first to die. Odin has promised a place by his side when true Scandinavians will sing and tell tales of former battles and achievements.'*

*'I myself have heard of this also from the bloodfathers, a series of apocàlyptic events some of which have already taken place will define the end of the world as we know it.'*

I added one last sentence to Redwald's predictions, *'the giants of frost and fire will come together to aid us in our fight supporting the true gods in one final engagement that will ultimately destroy this earth, submerging it under water.'*

Redwald scratched his balding scalp as he studied the positioning of the sun.

*'This is not right,'* he said as he sat beside me. *'Unless we have been blown hundreds of leagues to the south we are not on course to beach 'Sea Slicer' at Lindisfarena, plus the fact as the day seems warm for the north-eastern coastline.'*

*'How can you tell,'* I enquired, not knowing if I could keep my father's pretence going, *'damnés to his secrets,'* I thought to myself. I felt guilty about leaving Redwald in the dark about our mission.

We sat together on the steering bench and talked. I asked Redwald, *'when our vessel sailed from Aarhus what was its purpose?'*

Redwald was no fool, he knew of father's intention of sailing south towards the land that once joined southern Britannica with Francia before the waters overflowed the soil that previously connected the two with one another. The gods, in their wisdom, chose to create a gigantic wave of water that carved its way through the soft chalky white hills of southern Britannica and the lands once inhabited by the Franks, thereby creating the channel.

Redwald knew of the god's intentions of separating Britannica with the rest of the mainland, but it was my next question that foxed him.

I looked directly into his eyes as I asked, *'when we Danes sail to other lands, what are our primary intentions?'*

Unsure how to respond, Redwald looked in the direction of the sea before answering, *'assuming you are not trying to trick me there are three distinct groups of Dane or as we collectively call ourselves, Scandinavians - the most common being those who left home to rape, plunder and murder; then we have those who seek far off lands to settle; and finally we have the traders, those who sell fish and whale oil in exchange for farming produce and other products.*

*Those considered trustful and worthy to settle in Southern Britain happily set up workshops to produce a vast array of bone cups, tableware, glass beads, pottery, drinking vessels, and antler combs, leather goods, jewellery, and cloth. Once they trust enough not to bite the hand that feeds them, the Viking blacksmiths and armourers produced weapons of war including swords, battle axes, and chainmail.'*

*'Is there no other group Redwald,'* I shrewdly enquired.

*'I don't think so,'* he replied, still trying to think.

*'Well, today I will tell you there is a fourth group, one of which you are a member.'* Redwald looked at me in astonishment, but remained silent. *'We are undertaking a voyage of discovery, as you have already guessed our destination is not to be Lindisfarena but a harbour much further south and west.'*

*'Our beaching is to be on the coast of Dornsaete where we are to meet the young Prince Egbert of Wessex these are my instructions from my father.'*

Redwald suddenly looked afraid, he was nervous, and his face drained from its natural colouring.

*'Don't worry,'* I said, attempting to reassure him, *'we will not remain in Dornsaete, we are to travel north-east to the royal mint at Wilton,'* I sensed Redwald looked upon Dornsaete and Wilton with trepidation.

*'What about Malmesbury,'* he asked in trepidation; he looked fearful and terrified about the prospect of beaching 'Sea Slicer' at Waymouthe sands. I had never seen him look this way before; it was totally out of character. My friend and uncle half opened his mouth, but said nothing; his body trembled as he clumsily raised his hands to obscure his eyes, not from the sun, Redwald was utterly petrified of something, he was obviously in a state of severe shock.

I am no expert in body language, but it seemed to me that Redwald desired nothing more than to protect himself from something in his past, something presumably connected with Dornsaete.

Redwald was never a songster, even when drunk, however he tonelessly screeched out a song - *'I spy'd three ships come sailing by, come sailing by, come sailing by.*

After his dreadful attempt at singing he fell to his knees and cried like a baby.

I stood alongside my friend, utterly perplexed; why was Redwald singing a Christian song, could it be the songs origins were Norse and the Christian had foully infected them with their own beliefs.

I thought about our festivals - how we brought decorated trees inside our homes, as well as mistletoe, Yuletime, eggs and rabbits; every last one had been filched by the Christians.

I knew the roots of Christianity had been deliberately interlaced with our pagan traditions; since the Christian Church only gained strength through conversions.

Most of our sacred sites had been desecrated by the Christians who sacrificed mother earth to support the building of their churches.

Today, the Christians protest vehemently at the way we sack their monasteries, steal their trinkets and make slaves of their monks, those who are worth enslaving. The weak, undernourished and the elderly we throw into the sea. The value of Christian slaves was next to nothing, it was better to put an end to their miserable existence than offer them food and water. Most of them were incapable of sustaining a sea voyage. We are doing the Christians are favour by killing most of them and keeping a couple of the younger monks for their own amusement.

The Christians kill our captured Danish brothers in the most vilest and brutal of manners, the worst being what they call crucifixion, where a living man is nailed to a cross and left to die.

The Christians can't have it both ways!

Some of the crew gathered around Redwald in an attempt to bring him out from his nightmare, but my steersman kept rambling on about three ships.

What was the importance of these three ships? Redwald was not a man of faith, I wondered if he had seen a bloodfather prior to sailing. Sometimes sailors do that kind of thing in the hope of bringing them back safely into the arms of their loved ones.

I had seen the fear and revulsion in Redwald's eyes; but I hasten to say never in another human. The evil I witnessed one morning was similar to that which I had experienced in my own past. The very thought of it disturbs my mind to this day. I forever force my eyes to shut tight in the hope that my memory would swiftly fade the apparition I longed to forget, I had been branded on that day for I had perceived what can only be described as the extremities of malicious evil.

For the briefest of moment, I shut my eyes tight as I longer could bear evoke that foul vision again, but it wasn't a vision, the terror was real, and I couldn't bring myself to stare again into those repugnant drooling eyes or focus on that rabid frothing jaw, as the wolf was about to pounce and make its kill.

I was only four at the time, I was sent to collect water from a nearby stream; my father walked alongside me for company when suddenly we both spotted the rabid wolf. My instincts told me to scamper and run, but my father told to me make my stand. The wolf detected the odours of fear about my body. My leggings automatically became stained with piss and shit. My father lifted his axe and as the depraved creature came closer he sliced the wolfs head from its shoulders.

When we returned home, carrying the wolf head in a sack, my father told me the tale of Fenrir the wolf, and how the gods of Asgard had raised this wolf in order to stop him from wreaking havoc throughout the nine kingdoms, but Fenrir grew quickly and caused too much trouble that the gods decided to chain the creature up.

The gods convinced Fenrir to let them chain him up by pretending they were playing a game to see how strong he was, but Fenrir easily broke the chains. Eventually the gods had the dwarves make an exceptional chain that was stronger than anything known to man. But Fenrir was deeply suspicious about the chains and insisted that one of the god's voluntary put his hand in Fenrir's mouth while he was being chained as a sign of good faith. The god Tyr agreed to this, even though he knew he would lose his hand.

When Fenrir realised he had been tricked, he did indeed bite the hand of Tyr. Meanwhile the gods chained him to a boulder and placed a sword in his jaw to keep it open. The ensuing drool formed a foamy river known as *'Expectation'*.

I was so engrossed in my story telling that I forgot about my other duties.

A commotion at the prow of *'Sea Slicer'* swiftly brought me back to reality and my dilemma regarding Redwald.

Redwald and I sat together on his steering bench as I struggled to study his face, I tried to come to terms with his sudden and unexpected altering into something or someone I no longer knew or recognised.

Whatever it was that had distressed Redwald, it brought me back to the time when my father had saved me from Fenrir's jaw. I know that young boys of four are prone to exaggerate the truth, but I was the son of a Jarl and as such should have known better, a point my father continuously reminded me off.

I needed to unearth the answer to Redwald's torments, and uncover it soon. We sat on *Sea Slicer's* steering bench when again I remembered clearly apparition of a four year old boy and a rabid wolf who was about to steal this young boy's life.

As we sailed passed the Seven Sisters on our starboard bow, I heard grumbling noises from the crew, *'we ain't sailing to Lindisfarena,'* they cried in anguish.

Ever since Redwald had been aroused to my father's deception he had hidden himself away under the spare hessian sheet stowed neatly in the prow atop of the anchor. The crew had struggled to make some kind of conversation with him, but the only sound received in return was that of water being unceremoniously sliced by Sea Slicer bow wave, and occasionally the sound of Redwald pissing into our bilge. He had been there for four days and since then he had neither taken the opportunity to eat nor drink.

We knew he was alive due to the unpleasant sound of him farting and belching as he remained safely hidden away within his self-made territory.

If Redwald was unwilling to talk then that was fine by me, but my replacement young steersman kept asking questions that I could not in all honesty answer.

Stigsen was no more than fourteen years of age; and already had the look of a hardened seaman, his weather-beaten tanned face and hardened calloused hands, that only long stretches of holding the steering arm gave his trade away.

His long flowing blonde curly hair and the beginning of what looked like fluffy cat-fur beard made him look older than he was; for such a young lad he had learnt the skill of the steersman amazingly quickly, and what was fundamental in Stigsen young inexperienced mind - the maidens adored him.

When I enquired who had taught him his skill he answered Redwald, I should have known better than to ask such a question.

I gave him a light tap on the shoulder which was my way of showing gratitude to him and his master, I was truly gladdened to see his face lighting up with appreciation, for it was rare these days for a captain to praise a crewmember or show any act of decency toward his crew, unless it was a steersman, which I suppose he now was, due to Redwald absence.

I remained troubled by Redwald sudden change of character; why and what had transformed him so rapidly into becoming a meagre shadow of the giant of a man he once was. I kept thinking about our last conversation but nothing I had said should have brought about his abrupt change. I recalled speaking of not sailing to Lindisfarena, but he knew of this already. I told him our true destination was to be Dornsaete on the southern coast of Britain, where we would be welcomed by King Ealhmund. The king had his royal mint located within the old market towns of Wilton; the town was located there at a strategic point in the river systems of southern Wiltshire.

Redwald's response had only been *'Malmesbury'*, but why should Malmesbury be of great concern to him. I knew next to nothing of the place except it had been a long established place of learning and worship. A large Christian Abbey had been built there, towering over the countryside like a sentinel to their Christian God. Other than that there was nothing to fear about the damned place.

Could it be our proposed rendezvous with Prince Egbert of Wessex might have unnerved him, but I couldn't see why? There was nothing new in talking peace before going to war.

I knew nothing of the prince beyond his relationship with King Eahlmund and his bizarre claim of tracing his ancestry back to Cerdic - the founder and first king of all of Wessex. If either Egbert or Eahlmund felt the need to make either of them important in the eyes of a Jarl's youngest son, then so be it.

I slapped my legs hard to get the blood circulating deep inside my wet, cold and stiff limbs before I carefully stood, to fall would be an embarrassment.

Nothing made sense, and as far as I was aware Redwald had never sailed this far south before. The south coast of Britain was new to him, he had no reason to be troubled, but troubled he was!

Whatever troubled Redwald would have to wait until the sickness within his head subsided?

# CHAPTER FOUR

*"Fear not death for the hour of your doom is set and none may escape it."*

From the Volsunga Saga

Stigsen remained at his new post holding the steering arm as tightly as he could in case I decided to relieve him of his fresh duties, which I wouldn't even if Redwald recovered from his illness.

I ordered Stigsen to navigate to the south Wihtware, or as the Romans preferred to call the small insignificant island - Vectis Isle. It is said that the Britannica channel, at sometimes would prove difficult and strenuous to navigate but today the channel seemed unusually calm.

I told Stigsen of one of my father's voyages in the southern channel; it was a time when he needed to journey from the relatively unimportant fishing village of Dofras to sail to the far off western lands at Connibeare, he would then manoeuvre due north in the direction of Afon Hafre and finally onwards to Walentia. Jarl Thorgilssen wanted to know if the stories he had often heard of the Mercian King Offa were true or just illusionary nonsense. Legend are sometimes based on truth, but what my father wanted knowledge of was that of King Offa himself who apparently had grown weary of continuous cross boarder hostilities from the Saesonin warriors inside Walentia; he deemed he had no choice but to build an enormous structure, known as Clawdd Offa, to keep the Wealh scitte out from Mercia.

Thorgilssen left Dofras in Eastre; the weather had been abnormally hot and dry for that time of year, and towards the mid-afternoon the heat became unbearable, it left the crew restive. Suddenly there was a great stillness in the air when everything became silent as the grave. This was what the Britain's often called the lull before the storm; next the wind evoked a tremendous storm that blew with the ferocity like a herd of red deer stampeding out of control; hail stones began descending and swiftly filled our bilge, which afterwards smashed our timbers and shredded our sail. The waters rapidly turned foamy white before the rain fell in torrents; having lost five warriors overboard, one of which we managed to drag back over the gunnel, as we hurriedly turned the ship around and headed back to the safe waters of Aarhus.

Stigsen looked at me in amazement, wondering if my tale was true or was I teasing him.

To his surprise I told him - *'The wicked flee when no one is pursuing, but the righteous are bold as a lion.'* which made no sense to the young lad, which I suppose was true, especially as the words came from within the Christian book known as a bible. Although I intended the words to e a cautionary tale, Stigsen was none the wiser even though my words were true.

I ordered Stigsen to navigate *Sea Slicer*, closer to the island's bleak southern coastline, and advised him to be wary of the undersea rocks, as in the past these turbulent waters had devoured many a fine ship that floundered on its rugged coastal rocks, that added an additional fortification to the islands already formidable defences.

I thought it best to have a man forward with a weighted line checking our depth of water, *'if the depth is less than six horse hands deep - shout loud.'*

I peered ahead to the vast emptiness of the distant horizon when Stigsen drew my attention to large driftwood beacons which were never lit unless imposing danger approached. The beacons stood guard, like sentinels, along the entire length of the coastline of southern Britain, however on this day the beacons were being hastily made ready for firing. I could clearly see men on shore carrying large lit tapers in readiness to fire the beacons.

We had the King's official document of invitation, the seal of King Ealhmund himself had remained unbroken as I received it, and I had placed the document inside my leather tunic as proof of our being a friendly trading ship. Speaking to no one in particular I shouted above the noise of the sea, *'we should be welcomed, and not threatened in this way!*

We didn't carry that many weapons and those we had, if it came down to a real fight would be swiftly taken from us, and probably we would be put to the sword.

*'Better to be a living feign than a dead hero.'*

Redwald appeared out of nowhere to stand by my side. I had forgotten about him these past three days, but he abandoned the safety of his interim sheeted home from which had chose to hide; he began bellowing orders to the crew such as,

*'Make more sail,'*

The crew went about their duties with renewed vigour, springing into action, rushing to follow Redwald's commands; we began altering our guide ropes shifting them from one cleat to another.

Redwald twisted his huge neck to glare down on poor Stigsen, *'bend those muscles on the steering arm; we will need additional sea room between us and the coastline,'* Redwald distorted facial features angrily stared at me, *'and order the crew to cheer at the top of their voices, make those fucking warriors ashore; tell them to shout, applaud and make as much noise as possible; do everything you would do if you thought you were about to embrace a long lost brother; just let them buggers on the island think we are excited to meet with them and we are simple peaceful traders seeking only a brief refuge to beach Sea Slicer on one of their sandy beaches to trade our goods; it's about time we scrubbed them barnacles off.'*

I swiftly became aware of Redwald's supreme brilliance in drilling the crew and bellowing his repetitive orders; and their responses came from prolonged practice which had not gone unnoticed.

Keep a crew busy and they will forget all their worries they felt deep within their bones.

I shouted to the men to be vigilant, *'keep an eye on the horizon, make sure there are no other vessels in the channel this morning, shout to me, be them friend or foe.'*

I suddenly thought it could be possible we are not alone in sailing within the channel today. A Saxon ship could be sailing close inshore guarding against any approaching ship. Perhaps the beacons were to be lit in readiness for our arrival, a welcoming gesture.

At the time it seemed a rational answer as to why our sighting had caused the men ashore to lose their nerve, but I suppose this would be their first sighting of a Viking longboat.

I unceremoniously shoved Redwald forward to the prow; as I had so many questions requiring answers. Redwald had never, in all our sailing days, seen me like this. I was full of anger and fury and couldn't care less what he or the crew thought of my actions. I had the right to know what Redwald was keeping from me, especially if it placed the ship or the crew in mortal danger.

Initially Redwald conversed only in ambiguous riddles, it was only when he shouted *'Streð Mik,'* that his distorted face malformed into a ghastly shade of white, the veins about his face swiftly took on a bluish tinge and forehead rapidly became covered in globules of oily sweat, his eyebrows tightened, and his mouth half-open in readiness to talk, but once again not a sound came from his lips.

Redwald had taken on unmistakable appearance of terror intertwined with foreboding, as though it was branded upon his forehead. His frightening reactions steadily grew as I once more attempted to question him; but he remained a man who had lost his senses and his self-control. He became agitated and flustered by my repeated questioning. Finally I thought it best to have some crew sit quietly with him, hopefully they would be able to stabilise him.

Solveig and Torrun gently led Redwald away, my friend looked like a lamb to the slaughter, I felt guilty by his treatment by my hand; I became troubled by his unexplained circumstances and quietly advised the two young warriors to, *'report directly to me with every word he mutters while he remains in this present state of confusion and dread, it matters not how significant you might consider it to be, just come back and report all he tells you.'*

I did not have to wait that long before Torrun swiftly returned to give his short account, *'Redwald keeps repeating two names as well as repeating that damn Christian song about three boats sir.'*

*'What names lad,'* I impatiently enquired.

*'Tyr and Balor,'* Torrun replied, completely unaware of their significance or meaning

Could this be yet another sign from the gods; from the instance I received my father's sailing orders, nothing had gone to plan. First we had to endure that strange watery fog that left us imprisoned within its eerie grasp; secondly, we suffered an almighty storm where we all had witnessed demonic dragons dancing in the moonlit night sky; then rocks being thrown upon our heads, and today, just as we appear to be close to our destination we find our presence is not welcome.

Why should Loki treat us this way, unless Loki was not the cause?

I knew the legends and myths told of Tyr and Balor. Tyr was the Anglo-Saxon god of war; and was always assumed to be their greatest warrior god; it was Tyr, who was said to be their fiercest fighter, but he had one handicap - Tyr only had one hand, however he remained their most skilled and decorated warrior among the Anglo-Saxon gods. If it came to a battle, Tyr would always be found in the front rank of their shieldwall; Tyr was additionally their god of justice.

I couldn't reconcile the two, why was a god of war associated with a god of justice; the two are incompatible.

The Saxons continually described us as *"wolves among sheep"*. I personally considered the expression as an insult, but father simply brushed my words aside as though sweeping a speck of dust from his ceremonial tunic. Father had constantly spoken words of peace, especially as we were former allies.

It is true that our repeated raiding along Britain's coastline severly ravished the newly acquired land of the Saxon, but you have to bear in mind that the Angle-Saxon-Jute alliance had previously expelled the true Britain's from their land. Today there is next to nothing known of their culture, customs or ancient rites, our knowledge of them has been restricted to their bizarre stone circles that have been scattered throughout the length and breadth of the island. Our psychic's have always told us never, under any circumstances, should we seek refuge or enter any of these peculiar stone circles as they thought them to be inhabited by the ghosts of Balor and his followers, who although dead, his bones once again return to this life because his sacred resting place had been desecrated.

Innocent captives from bordering tribes have been sacrificed in the name of Balor. A particular nasty form of sacrifice adopted by his cult is known as *'hung meat,'* whereby his followers pierce the heels of their victim and thereafter thread ropes through the piercing, and finally upend the victim before leaving them to die.

Not only was the piercing of the heels horrendously painful, the victim's blood ran down thereby covering the bare chest of the afflicted with their own blood.

To my mind the *'blood eagle'* was nothing more than a symbolist obnoxious form of implementing an execution - sacrificial rites were never intended; only the purity of a sacrifice in the name of a specifically named god to be honoured would suffice, those human beings sacrificed must of been young and pure and always a virgin; unless the sacrifice to be offered in the name of the goddess 'Hel.' She would welcome a warrior from an opposing tribe to her ravenous hell.

Executions seldom appease the gods. How could the gods be pleased when the victim was executed? If you are to be executed then you are an evil and bad person, execution is a verdict proclaimed by man. Only the gods could order a killing.

In the *'blood eagle'* the victim was placed in a prone position, their ribs severed from the spine by means of sharp blade, their lungs were pulled through the opening created thereby giving the illusion of a pair of *"wings"*.

The gods, even the Christian's told tales of human sacrifice; we were informed that a prophet named Abraham was ordered by his God to sacrifice his first born son just to prove his faith.

*'If this was true, we were completely Føkka'.*

Springtime in Jutland was nothing more than a distant memory to us, but we all gradually came to terms with the repeated tormenting visions observed by us all in the night sky; especially those apparitions that occurred experienced in the northern desolate cold lands of Bernica. We heard rumour of immense whirlwinds, flashes of lightning and fiery dragons seen flying in the pitch darkness of the blackened night sky, all of which were not that dissimilar to those we witnessed ourselves when attempting to sail in the vast expanse of the Great Northern Ocean. The Anglo-Saxons looked upon these signs as omens from their gods of a foreboding catastrophe.

The stone circle at Stonehenge

Odin had predicted, since the beginning of time, of a harvest season blighted by famine and deprivation; his prophecy told of the demise of an ancient civilisation of warriors that once roamed these shores. Balor, the evil one, brought about an immense scarcity of food in which not only did man endure but also his beasts suffered and died.

Britannica would bear the brunt of Balor's wrath whereby the land would remain poisoned and die for many seasons. Balor and his horde remained unseen living beneath the filth they called skáli. If by chance the harvest succeeded, Balor pledged to return and devour in one night whatever crops remained.

I knew of Balor's reputation as being a ravenous, vile and despicable god after reading ancient scrolls my brothers brought home with them after raiding the shores of Britannica.

Balor was the undisputed ruler of the repugnant and gruesome underworld, where the most abominable creatures that ever lived on land, sea or in the air came from. Balor was particularly gruesome load of shit living beneath the ground to wreak hazard on us mortals.

Balor had one magical malicious eye which was undeniably his greatest weapon against humans; just one glance from his demonic solitary eye would kill you!

*'The ghosts of Celtic Britain had seemingly created a war between the Anglo-Saxon-Jute coalition and we Vikings, and as sailed speaking words of peace and reconciliation,'* Balor and his devilish were stirring up trouble to bring about a war, possibly a war that would end with no human remaining alive.

Whilst I sat contemplating what malevolence surrounded us Torrun remained by my side.

*'Redwald sang of three ships in his song,'* Torrun, continued with his brief report in a hushed voice

*'But we are just one,'* I said, trying not to cause alarm.

When unexpectedly the seaman on lookout cried out, *'two sails on the western horizon.'*

Everyone twisted around to look west - two ships! I judged the distance between us and them to be no more than twenty nautical rôst away. If I was right we should pass each other in the time it takes for a warrior to humps a captive slave.

*"I spy'd three ships come sailing b*

# CHAPTER FIVE

*"Don't ever make any promises you don't intend to keep.*
*God Tyr wouldn't have had to sacrifice his hand*
*without the oath breaking deeds of Gods.*
*Ragnarok wouldn't have had to happen if God's*
*hadn't gone back on their words.*
*Bitter but true though."*

From The Saga of Hrafnkel Freysgothi.

As the two longboats sailed ever closer it was plainly obvious from the dragon figureheads they were Norse, and probably part of a much larger Viking raiding party. As soon as we were within hailing distance they explained the longboats had sailed from southern Ériú in the hope of raiding Anglo-Saxon lands within Dornsaete and Dumnionii coast. I described of our growing misfortunes and our intention to beach Sea Slicer somewhere Dornsaete to carry out important repairs and raid a local village of food to assist us in our returning; I added our stay had to be short, it was our intention to return to the Kattegat Sea before the dragon fish Jormungandr caught the scent of our blood.

The crews from each ship exchanged hearty gestures band cheering as they sailed past; we wished them good sailing and not to steal everything as we desperately required sufficient to return home.

I could not help but notice in the prow of each longboat stood a berserker, an ugly and unruly warrior who worshiped Odin, they normally attach themselves to a royal and noble court as bodyguards or shock troops. I had not considered the longboats belonged to royal blood.

Within the time it takes for a famished man to eat his breakfast, a beserker would kill or maim twenty men who opposed him.

We remained motionless to the west of Weymouth Bay our anchor gripping the underwater rocky beach. The water shone like sparkling crystals, all seemed calm, but no more than a mile away in Weymouth Bay the beserkers were doing what they do best. I visualised two boatloads of Viking warriors, jostling and jumping into the break-waters as they each tried to be the second man ashore; he would be the first to sample the local ale, and second to savour the maidens puse, and the second to thieve from the monks all the trinkets hidden away inside their the Christian church. No doubt the Abbot would try to keep them from finding such trinkets; but the monks always found great difficulty in finding novel hiding places to keep their riches safe from the Vikings.

Throughout the decades, our battle strategy had been - havoc, ale, whores and a good death. If that plan worked, which it normally did, there was no reason for change; unless, like today, Weymouth had been so well garrisoned, that before sunset the invaders who stood their ground were now languishing, below ground within a rat infested, damp, murky, inhospitable, Anglo-Saxon dungeon, the berserkers hadn't lived long enough to carry out their shock tactics.

Later, when everything had calmed, the separate pieces of the day came together, and in doing so the child's puzzle had been completed, or in this case - how the Vikings had been defeated by superior odds.

King Ealhmund's reeve had informed the king of an imminent plot to assassinate the King, but they had no idea in what direction the plot came from, but the Saxons had little doubt we Norsemen would be the likely cause of any treachery, and the Danes would be held accountable for their deceitfulness.

I suppose strictly speaking we couldn't call our fellow seamen as prisoners' or survivors because every last one of them was dragged from whatever brothel they happened to spend their coin before being overcome and detained until King Ealhmund decided upon their fate.

Hearing the news of the farcical attempt to assassinate Eahlmund, he immediately flew into an uncontrollable rage whereby without thinking of the consequences he decided to kill every Dane living within Wessex boundaries, which included all those who had already settled peacefully farming the land. Eahlmund forgot that the Vikings might return in number to avenge their countrymen, and the King would be the first to suffer vengeance.

The Norsemen had been ravenously eating food and drinking in the town's alehouses; perhaps the uninvited men were not so quiet, but you get the picture. The intruders were swiftly removed by order of King Eahlmund to be detained within the kings holding house before being forcibly conveyed to Oxnaford. It was ludicrous to believe the prisoners' true aim was to slit the throats of the King and all his male heirs, it just was unthinkable.

The King Eahlmund decreed by proclamation drawn up by his scribes -

*"For it is fully agreed that to all dwelling in this country it will be well known that, since a decree was sent out by me with the counsel of my leading men and magnates, to the effect that all the Danes who had sprung up in this island, sprouting like cockles amongst the wheat, were to be destroyed by a most just extermination, and thus this decree was to be put into effect even as far as death, those Danes who dwelt in the afore-mentioned town, striving to escape death, entered*

*this sanctuary of Christ, having broken by force the doors and bolts, and resolved to make refuge and defence for themselves therein against the people of the town and the suburbs; but when all the people in pursuit strove, forced by necessity, to drive them out, and could not, they set fire to the planks and burnt, as it seems, this church with its ornaments and its books. Afterwards, with God's aid, it was renewed by me.*

The Christians honoured the day by naming it after one of their saintly feast day's *'Saint Brice's day,'* but as long as blood flowed through the veins of Vikings we knew it as *'The Slaughter of the Innocents'*, and as it is our right to wreck vengeance on those who take a Dane life outside of battle, it is our sacred right, by the almighty Odin, to take our vengeance on those responsible.

In consequence to the violent Saxon punishment and barbarism, retribution was swift and true. The Norsemen relentlessly savaged Saxon coastal lands of Britain. However there was a drawback regarding our frequent incursion; for we had accumulated too many Anglo-Saxon slaves that they no longer held any significant value to our Frankish brothers across the channel.

After the Romans departed Britain for mainland Europe, the formidable Franks established themselves as the major, all powerful, conquering force, but we Vikings remained content being their trading partners.

There had always been a code of honour between the Franks and Viking, and despite our continuous warlike situation many Vikings sold themselves as mercenaries in Frankish campaigns.

But once we began raiding the Frankian heartland, the code of honour that had previously existed to hold our two great enterprises in peace swiftly disintegrated; I think this was inevitable, when two equals try to come together, neither one is overly encouraged to play the underdog. In consequence of our squabbling we eventually went our separate ways. We continued raiding the weakly defended towns and monasteries, but we never again as a united force.

Yuletide came and went and I could see with my own eyes the crew had become restless, those with families counselled me to return home to Aarhus and the crystal clear waters of the Kattegat Sea; those free to choose if they we stayed or remained felt an overcoming attraction to return home. They had enough gold and silver in their pockets to last them many summers, unless they became foolish and found a second wife.

Women were costly to keep content these days!

Redwald had recovered sufficiently from his head sickness although he was never truly responsive and affable to me as we had been. We had once been happy to call ourselves blood-brothers. We knew each other's minds prior to our utterance, but now he remained distant, but I still thought of him as kin.

True to my word we sailed for home once the springtime sowing season was over, the early flowers changed the landscape into a mirage of countless colours. We left the Dornsaete coast and sailed for home to be once more with family and friends. Wihtware proved to be a dismal uninspiring place to plunder; it appeared only to support the grazing of animals and the only thing you might call rich was the islands green pastures. We might have grown fat and lazy by eating an abundant supply of pig, sheep and cattle but due to the fact finding nature of our voyage we lacked the treasurer our ancestors sang about.

I must confess if Torrun had gained additional weight his leggings barely fastened together.

The southern coastline of the British Isles proved exceptionally rocky and hilly, much like home but without the snow and ice. I enjoyed this time of peace to restore my inner self.

Redwald gradually returned to normality but I promised Stigsen to be our permanent steersman.

Redwald appeared unbothered by my choice, as I had promoted my friend to be the sailing master, leaving me additional time to study the coastline of southern Britain to draw maps where I would add the names of various coastal towns and villages, particularly those that might pose a threat to us if we launched an attack from either the south or the east; any assault from the north of Britain would have to first contend with the unruly fierce warriors of Alba. A fiercesome warrior had already proclaimed himself king in Ireland.

The Vikings had proclaimed themselves masters of all they surveyed in Ireland.

The longer the Saxons allowed the Danes to settle in Britain, with the passing of the seasons they would find the interlopers would be hard to remove from the townships and villages of Saxon Britain.

The Saxons had constructed robust defences surrounding their towns, and disciplined the peasants, in time of conflict, to protect their filthy hovels; it is strange to see what an opponent will fight for. But what stood out in my mind was that these southern Wessex and Mercian Saxon's seldom took advantage of making use of the stone materials discarded by the Romans after they turned-tail and ran back to wherever their homeland might be.

*'I say good riddance to bad rubbish!*

As we sailed home I wondered if anything in Aarhus had altered; I doubted if any of my brothers had learnt the true art of warfare, and I couldn't wait to show my father the maps I had drafted of the south and eastern coastline of the British Isles. I had carefully marked every creek, river and stream that flowed inland from the channel and the Northern Ocean; these drafts would prove invaluable once the Council decided to attack.

Stigsen wanted to return home for he had married his childhood sweetheart one full moon prior to our sailing, his fellow crewmembers were teasing him how many children he might return home to.

The crew were thrilled to be sailing home, their high spirits and gaiety flowed in abundance, the sound of laughter rang out inside the modest space within *Sea Slicer's,* everyone was smiling and jovial; that is everyone with the exception of Redwald. He seemed lost inside his gloomy thoughts; no longer did he seek the company of others, he scarcely spoke of the events leading up to our anchoring off Weymouth Bay or the unexpected sighting of two fellow Viking longboats.

Solitude was his lone companion!

But I needed Redwald by my side, I refused to give up on the man I had respected my entire life. He was the man who roused the crew at the time of our greatest want.

Redwald was like a second father to me, or as the converted Anglo-Saxons called them - a Godfather. I needed Redwald more than anything in the world. He was my talisman, my lucky charm and my salvation; I could explain things to Redwald that I found difficult to explain to my father. Redwald had listened and understood my problems when father found my ideas over complicated. If we were to attack the British shoreline from the south or the east I had to have Redwald alongside me.

I had to pass through the shutters Redwald had closed to everyone, including me. But if I had to break through his barricades to enter his mind - so be it, break them I must do!

Loviatar the blind daughter of Tuoni
The goddess of death and disease

# CHAPTER SIX

*"Where you recognise evil, speak out against it, and give no truces to your enemies"*

From the Hávamál or the Sayings of Odin

As we entered our home port the pungent overpowering odour of fish filled the quayside; a mere breeze would fill our lungs with its repulsive stench that perpetually loitered in the air we breathed, choking anybody who lingered too long on the quayside.

What a beautiful welcome I thought, as we sailed through the outer arms of Aarhus harbour walls. The convivial sound of giant horns blew honouring our safe return, as the sun-kissed morning radiance brought down to earth by the gods poured upon us from the heavens. The glittering reflections upon the water reached out to guide us throughout the final stages of our voyage; we each felt the pangs of home touch us as we rowed those final indulgent moments. We each scanned the distant quayside as we seeked for our loved ones.

Nothing had changed; the sound of harmonious fisher songs heralded our arrival; with anticipation our wives, mothers and sweethearts stood to greet their loved ones. Most dreamed of this moment, scarcely thinking it would ever come true, for some boats never returned leaving their loved ones bereft of not knowing or understanding the reason.

Stigsen was the first man to jump ashore, in his excitement he must have cleared over two horse lengths as he twisted and turned trying to look for his wife, the rest of the men pushed and jostled each other swiftly followed Stigsen example.

Stigsen landed on his rear end causing him to yelp like baby in pain, he eventually got to both feet but she didn't seem to be on the quayside; he turned again and to his delight she was there standing directly in front of him, babe in arms. The incessant teasing he had put up with throughout our voyage stopped as the congratulatory slaps pounded on his head and shoulders, as Stigsen smiled.

Redwald was hanging back, knowing no one would be there to welcome him home. Witnessing his dilemma I placed my arm about his shoulders and softly told him, *'come let us see what my father has to say about the bounty we have brought home,'* however I secretly became excited if he approved of my map making.

The sudden realisation hit me full in the face, as I marvelled at the spectacular sites and reflected on the enchanted wonderland of attractions that would greet us as we walked together to my Thorgilssen Hall.

We stopped just short of the massive entrance, the hall had been highly decorated with all sorts of paraphernalia; *'surely this welcome is not just for me,'* I puffed out my cheeks and smiled with pride.

A gruff voice behind me replied, *'by the Gods, look what Jormungandr has dumped by our porch.'*

It was my brother dressed in his finest tunic and cleans leggings, his hair had been trimmed and platted; Pedersen, at best, looked like of a sack of grain tied in the middle. *'By the Gods,'* I was lost for words!

*'Is our father well?'* I eventually found the courage to ask, *'I thought, by the way you are dressed, you are about to celebrate his funeral.*

*'He is well little brother,'* Pedersen cautiously replied, *'I have great news - for today I am to marry and you little turd are to toast our happiness.'* I rushed forward to embrace my brother kissing him on both checks. Since the day I had been born Pedersen had

only teased me, but I loved him, he had taught me everything about wood craft and how to survival alone in the woodland surrounding Albaek Bay. Once he knew of my lucky escape from the rabid wolf he taught me how to defend myself from the other wolves.

*'That is what brothers are for little kid.'* Pedersen had never called me by my given name, but always as *"kid."*

Marriage, in our culture, is at the heart of the family structure - hence the intricate nature of our wedding rituals; before planning the wedding ceremony certain traditions must be complied with even if you consider them to be time-consuming, it begs the question, why do we get married?

Pedersen looked perplexed as he answered -

*'The first question is always - who has the most time on their hands? According to our myths and folklore, the wedding ritual is deemed essential to earn the rewards and blessings of the gods; which of course is an important step on the path to parenthood, and to continue our bloodline.*

*A Viking marriage ceremony is not just a union between couples; it is a union between families. Therefore, the wedding observance has to be a long drawn-out process. Various negotiations have to be conducted before the terms of the marriage can be formally agreed upon. At the commencement of the marriage procedure, the groom's family, along with his legal representatives must meet to determine the size of the bride's dowry, together with the negotiation concerning wedding gifts to be sent by the groom's parents. Once settled the groom's financial assets has to be approved, before the date of the actual wedding is agreed.*

*In the lead up to a wedding, the bride and groom are separated to enable them to wash away their earlier life before being allowed to live as one.*

*The bride has to be stripped of all her old clothing, together with every symbol associated with her unwed status is discarded, the only exception being her head wreath or gilt circlet normally worn by unmarried maidens, this is gently removed and retained for the marriage of their first daughter.'*

I was no more than an arm's length from my brother when I muttered these words -

*'You have no patience brother, why don't you just hump her to save time.'*

You should have seen Pedersen's face as he tried unsuccessfully to rearrange my face, but he did give me a vicious kick to the shin bone. The two of us scrapped, entwined in a bundle on the dirt floor beyond father's thresh-hold.

Upon hearing the commotion outside his hall my father came to investigate the cause, and seeing his two sons' play-fighting he decided to leave well alone.

*'Boys will be boys!'* he chuckled before retiring back inside his.

Redwald looked on in utter amazement as he witnessed two brothers pretending to throw blows at blows and knocks about the head.

*'Don't touch my face,'* Pedersen laughed in excitement, *'I am soon to be married. I don't want my wife seeing me with cuts and bruises about my pretty face.*

*'Who is the lucky girl,'* I chuckled in merriment; *'I hope it's not Ragner's daughter, she forever smells of blubber and every boy in the village has humped her at least twice.'* Swiftly realising the foolishness of my joke, I shoved my brother away to give distance between us; although I need not have worried as he burst into laughter. Tears of excitement rolled down his grubby face; and both of us could barely stand as we persisted in our stupidity; hearing the commotion outside I noticed my father looking down at us showing his intense disapproval at the antics of his two youngest

boys. *'Your mother would be mortified to see both of you romping about like two year olds.'*

This was true!

*'Grow up,'* father yelled, *'or I'll stick my seaux where the sun does not shine, you have disturbed my peace once too often, wedding or no wedding I will crack your idiotic head's together.'*

Both of us knew once father had been roused he was more than capable of carrying out his promises.

*'Father is in a bad mood today,'* Pedersen explained, *'I think this business at Lindisfarena is keeping him awake at night.'*

I stood to offer Pedersen my hand to assist his rising; he gave me a quick jerk of the arm and grinned as he again took my hand as we staggered, arm in arm, into the great hall.

Poor bedraggled Redwald didn't know if he should follow or not, but seeing me beckoning him to follow he readily joined us.

Father being the headman of the counsel it was his right to sit in the highly carved chair atop of the raised area to face his guests; my three elder brothers sat by close by his side while other dignitaries were seated according to rank about the tables where food and drink was about to be served.

Pedersen, Redwald and I carefully walked around the edge of the hall and took our places directly behind father. The assembled guests waited patiently for the three of us to take our seats before my father pounded the table with the handle of his ceremonial axe thereby bringing the counsel meeting to order.

The noise within the great hall steadily grew; as each family shouted trying to put their views to the counsel; the talk of vengeance against the Anglo-Saxons in slaughtering Viking prisoners at Oxnaford was apparently the only item under discussion. *'We must send the Saxons a robust warning; a simple gesture will not carry any weight,'* an arseling towards the rear of the hall shouted. The tables were being battered with helmets and fists in support of the arselings proposition, the gathering was quickly getting out of control, although everyone seemed to agree, *'what form should the warning be,'* another shouted, *'and where should it take place.'*

The majority clearly thought it should be at either Mealdmesbyrig or Cyninges Tun; the latter being the border town standing between Wessex and Mercia; while others thought Colneceastre in Mercia would make the Saxons sit up to smell the stench of their turds.

*'What about Lindisfarena,'* my elder brother, Jour shouted, *'it is a very small island off the coast of Bernica,'* he yelled, *'we should kill everyone at Lindisfarena just as our Viking brothers were slaughtered at Oxnaford by the Saxon schitte.'* With the seed thus planted, the cheers once more prevailed.

Redwald stood to ask his question, *'if Lindisfarena is to be the target you must decide first on the tactics, do you intend killing every Christian living there, remember some still remain loyal the teachings of our old gods. If you seek only vengeance, the Saxons must first realise the grounds for your retribution, otherwise the true meaning of the assault might be misconstrued.'*

Redwald looked at me wondering if he should continue talking or retake his seat. Thinking Redwald's words to be wise, I beckoned him to continue, but his moment had gone as the invited assembly swiftly turned their back on misinterpretations.

*'What about the fort the Saxons have on the island?'* someone passionately shrieked.

Pedersen tried making his presence known by joining the debate, *'we must time the raid to correspond with the high spring tides, in this way the causeway will be part of time submerged leaving the island cut off from the mainland and reinforcements.'*

*'True,'* Redwald replied, *'this is a point we have to take into consideration, if the Lords vote for war.'*

I scrutinized Thorgilssen facial reactions as each counsel member cast their vote; it was difficult to judge if the Jarl was in favour of such a raid. The wisest members preached prudence, while the younger headstrong sought Saxon blood.

Father banged the pommel of his sword hard on the wooden flooring to signal silence.

A deafening hush swiftly returned, however a small minority persisted in crying out, however the glare on father's face quickly brought order and stillness to his hall.

*'The meeting is closed,'* he looked weary as he spoke passionately from the heart, *'you will have my decision by sunset tomorrow.'*

Afterwards I spoke with Redwald, to remind him, *'silence is such a wonderful thing, you cannot see it, hear it or touch it, and I suppose that's what makes it so special.'*

We wondered why something as negative as silence could literally take root and grow within the brains of these fools. The seed the counsel planted today of making Lindisfarena their priority will be nurtured and grown. An overwhelming feeling of emotion swelled within the great hall grew until the surge of passion, likened to the sound of breakers pounding the shingled shoreline of Saxon beaches.

With the exception of a few moderate thinking lords, Redwald and I, we anticipated the vote not going in our favour, if so war would soon be declared.

I sat down with my father, my four brothers and Redwald to explain my concerns.

*'Whatever the outcome might be with reference to Lindisfarena, one side or the other, be it Viking or Saxon, one will be brushed aside as if they had never existed.*

Redwald followed my lead by explaining, in his view it will be the end of both Saxon and Dane, he likened the coming events to the Romans departing Britannica's shore; Rome will never again return to our shores again as conquerors, for they are now the conquered.

Come morning, the chatter within our village was only of the forthcoming war, *'you would have thought the decision had already been made the way these boys speak,'* Pedersen spat the words, *'let's have breakfast,'* he continued, *'and afterwards I will show you the extended village; since you've been away we have had a considerable influx of new families anxious to join us.'*

The three of us sauntered off together, as we tried collecting our thoughts, Pedersen was the first to speak, *'the way those boys talk you would have thought they were going to war against a formidable enemy; instead they will practice their sword skills on a small group of timid, feeble minded, elderly men; the only thing the monks have ever held in their entire lives is probably a quill or brush.'*

*'True,'* I replied trying not to show my contempt to a group of boys we had just passed. *'They have never purposely killed another living creature in their wretched short lives; I suppose their mothers have to wring the necks of the chickens they wolf-down in the evenings.'*

Redwald looked solemn as we continued walking; and Pedersen was naturally downcast, due to his wedding being deferred until this business at Lindisfarena had been settled.

The three of us came to an unexpected stop as we gazed upon one of nature's unblemished beauty. I slowly pointed to a family of red foxes; the male briefly gazed in our direction before deciding we meant him no harm as he continued inhaling at something in the lush green meadow grass. Possibly another animal had either tried marking his territory or buried the leftovers a recent kill. He looked magnificent with his blazoned white chest, slightly flattened skull, upright triangular ears, and his pointed, slightly upturned snout, but what attracted him to me was his long highly coloured thick bushy brush. He purposely repositioned himself between the vixen and us; he persistently sniffed the ground and raised his head to detect if we meant him or his family any harm. There were only two youngsters within the family group, which I assumed meant others were hiding within the nearby wood or had the group been attacked leaving two pups to survive.

The three of us lingered mesmerized as we continued watching the pups peacefully playing without a care in the world.

The fox casually stared at us one final time before deciding to gather his little family into the nearby woodland, they might have disappeared from sight, but we heard a few friendly barks followed by a whistling sound, which we presumed were his gestures of amity.

I felt at peace in the meadow, the softness of lush green grass felt extremely comforting as we lay together on our backs; I briefly closed my eyes as I tried to recall the abundant colours of the numerous wild flowers each struggling to reach the light of the sun, blues, reds, yellows, whites and deep purples all tinged with gold from the suns natural rays. I could have remained in the meadow, listening to the sound of water flowing from the nearby stream; the constant humming noise of various insects flying close by my face did not bother me, I was at peace, like the fox we had just set our eyes upon.

I very quietly stood and looked down on Redwald and my brother, the two of them grunted in their sleep, or was that a snore?

I sighed; it was time to go back to Thorgilssen's great hall, to a peculiar form of reality where conflict and disputes should be settled by words, and not by the clashing of swords.

# CHAPTER SEVEN

*"If aware that another is wicked, say so:*
*Make no truce or treaty with foes."*

From the Hávamál or the Sayings of Odin

The Great Horn was blown, signalling a call to arms. The result of last evenings was evidently already known to everyone as we entered the great hall.

Father sat, grim faced in his raised chair as the various lords and families quietly took their seats; at least this gathering showed a greater respectability than the previous.

Father's hushed words echoed about the hall as he signalled the votes cast were in favour of war against the Anglo-Saxon. It was obvious for all to see, father had not slept during the night, his head ached from the demands placed on him as Jarl and head of the counsel; and the unmistakable sign of dark heavy circles beneath both eyes was somewhat of a giveaway.

Thorgilssen stood to declare, *'we will send a token force of three longboats and one hundred warriors in total to sail to the island known as Lindisfarena within the region of Bernica; our purpose there is to send a clear message to the Anglo-Saxons of our disapproval of murdering our Daneland brothers in Oxnaford. These boats will depart from our shores in the month of Skerpla, where the tides are favourable.*

*In addition to the three boats and one hundred carefully chosen warriors I will send a small party of observers, lead by my son, to record the events of your actions as truthfully as possible.'*

Father, looked drained and with considerable difficulty, tapped the edge of his sword on the table to signal the meeting was closed.

*Our assault at Lindisfarena cannot be likened to a game of Hnefatafl where one side or the other will be beaten, for I fear the great hall of Valhalla will forever be closed and its giant doors firmly bolted thus preventing our entrance.*

*Father, I freely admit having feelings of great sadness that Lindisfarena had been chosen as the target of our attack. I have only seen coloured drawings of this small green lush island. The formation of the amazing rock configuration at first view to be the building blocks of the giants; I could never see mankind able to construct such a beautiful dwelling place of solace that only the gods have made perfect. The isolated monastery island of*

*Lindisfarena might have brought us together, as one, the Christian's, the Anglo-Saxon alliance, and we Danes could have built an alliance that one day could, in time, ruled the world. But all that is gone, the dream is no more.*

*Lindisfarena is one of the holiest places in the Angel Isle, the Anglo-Saxon will defend the island to the last man; not even the wrath of our gods will help us if this new God of peace and harmony distracts us from the unholy path we have taken this day.*

*Christian Britain will fear Norsemen for a brief time, however others will believe our raid to be a message sent from the heavens by the Christian God. They will assume their god has forsaken them and they have been punished through none other than their faults. You must remember Lord; the Christians fervently believe in a great day of judgement, when all their sins will be washed away, just as our maidens wash away their earlier life prior to marriage. The Christian's believe in an afterlife when they come back from the dead to live again with their families. Be assured the Christians are many and we are but few.*

*Answer me this great Lord - will Valhalla welcome us if we are to be the ones responsible for the annihilation of the Viking race? I worry about the destruction of our culture, if we carry out the proposal to assault Lindisfarena#. We will be held answerable for our many crimes harvested in our lifetimes. I fear Christianity will prosper and grow, while our days and that of our gods are numbered. There will come a time when our gods will cease to exist, they will be forgotten, as this new god they call Yeshua will bring kingdoms together to unite in bringing about our downfall. Redwald has had a vision, he see's warriors dressed in white robes with a red cross about their breast.*

*He has heard rumours that the Christian God seeks blood for blood; I have heard with my own ears that their monks preach 'a life for a life, and an eye for eye.' They believe in a father figure, similar to Odin; they many have priests spread about this world. Unlike Odin they have a father-figure who dwells in a great city where the Caesars of Rome once lived.*

*They believe four horsemen will come as a symbolic warning to predict death and destructions upon our world, when the days of man will be no more; these horsemen represent famine, conquest, violence and death. We are all aware that three of these ciphers are the foundations by which we exist. I therefore strongly recommend that we do not sail to Lindisfarena with horses in our ships. If we're to attack the Christians it should only be on foot - do not consider fighting on horseback, finally we should not linger at Lindisfarena; as the vanquisher, our vengeance must be swift and decisive and we must quickly return home. I am told the Christian God has a long reach, he will seek those who have offended him, and there is talk that he kills the sons of those who cause him offence.*

After I had spoken father turned to look at me, *'do you truly believe what you have told us my son'*

I nodded my head in agreement, as did Redwald, for in his trance-state he felt himself in the presence of the Christian God, *'Redwald has had many dreams and visions relating to the old gods, they described the reasons why they fought between themselves in the great halls of Valhalla, apparently they never found a lasting peace within the vastness of the clouds.*

*Tuoni and Loviata, the evil ones, and their followers were forced out of Valhalla by Odin the Great. He reflected on a war between the gods as unimaginable; never the less the battle came and it raged on unresolved for years until the evil ones were defeated, some were slain and others were imprisoned by Thor.*

*The defeated demi-gods should have been slaughtered, but Odin, in his mercy merely banished Loviatar and Tuoni. For where goodness lives you must remember evil will always stir, and from that mixture of malicious obnoxious wasteland found only in black stars in the heavens the unjust will again try to bring about the fall of Odin and everything he stands for.*

*The evil ones have learnt from their mistakes although they vowed never to fight Odin's again, Tuoni and his bringer of death, the daughter Loviatar will ascend from the pits of hell to penetrate the hearts of those who carried out the injustice attack on Holy Island.*

*Odin and Thor do not wish us to initiate hostilities against the Anglo-Saxon until the time is right. Odin has befriended the Hebrew Yehoshua; he believes his cause to be just. If you seek war by going against Odin's wishes the Anglo-Saxon armies will within three centuries destroy us.'*

Thorgilssen thought long and hard before giving his answer, - *'then neither your brothers nor I will join the hostilities soon to bring destruction on British soil. Redwald will pray to the gods and reconcile our fate on our behalf, but I still ask you to sail with the fleet as an unarmed observer, those who sail this day must themselves answer to Odin's judgement.'*

Viking rune for strength

# Chapter Eight

*'The only sounds were that of the sea, our church bell and the gulls, but the assault upon our gentle lives was so sudden and brutal.'*

An account of the raid at Lindisfarne
by a surving monk.

Throughout the early months of the Christian year 793 Pagan and Christians alike warned of alarming times to come. The Anglo-Saxon scholars in the north wrote of immense whirlwinds, treacherous explosions of dazzling light and of evil dragons flying in the night sky. Every scholar reflected on their thoughts as this airborne phenomenon crashed down from the heavens signalling omens of calamities soon to come.

Our spies reported that on the twenty-third day of September, in the Christian year 788, an important secular Bernican nobleman named Sicga led a group of like minded conspirators, with the intention of assassinating King Ælfwald of Bernica. Once Sicga had carried out his deadly deed he quickly had feelings of deep lamentation and regret, but by then it was too late. Ælfwald's successor Lord Osred gave Sicga an offer; a choice of being killed as a traitor, or die by his own sword. Sicga chose to the latter and killed himself, what the Christians call a suicide; his body was afterwards, as assured by Lord Osred, laid to rest within the perimeter of Lindisfarena priory.

Ælfwald being the last of the Wuffingas from Norðfolc and Elklet, his body was carried to Hexham Abbey for burial.

The final plans of our assault on Lindisfarena on the north-east coast of Northanhymbre would be one of the most audacious raids the Vikings ever contemplated. Surprisingly the Vikings chose to keep the names of their leader's secret in fear of reprisals from the Christian God.

The plan was simple; tear down and dismantle every facet of their abhorrent Christian ideology and accomplishments with one prominent strike at their very heart of all their religious, creative, artistic and academic triumphs would crumble.

The two northern monasteries at Donaemuth and Monkswearmouth had previously blocked our advancement but if Lindisfarena fell the others must fall thereby extending the Danelaw in the north. This would leave Mercia's northern border constantly exposed to attack. Once Mercia fell, Wessex must, as sure as night follows day, capitulate and yield. Prince Egbert and King Ealhmund of Cent, the ruler in Wessex are feeble and weak; they could never defend Wessex against the might of our Viking warriors.

I was again beckoned to father's great hall apparently he required knowledge of events I had learnt appertaining to the continuous quarrelling between Offa and Ecgberht. For a brief time I stood and said nothing, I remained steadfast in my opposition to a raid at Lindisfarena. Father's anger and impatience spilled out, he wanted to know who ruled and where; he had no need of a history lesson regarding the Anglo-Saxons childish bickering. As far as he was concerned he wanted the name of the Anglo-Saxon king that dominated Britain

I informed him, *'whoever reigns in Wessex or Mercia, keep them apart and we stand a chance, but if they are united we will must surly lose.'*

I regained my composure, cleared my throat, and raised myself to my full height before explaining that in my humble opinion Ealhmund ruled in name only, his son Ecgberht considered himself to be the real power behind the throne. Wessex is in turmoil, and Mercia wish for nothing except a full independence from Wessex; the way they are acting during these past months I believe nothing but a civil war will ensue. However I stress caution, if our attack at Lindisfarena is carried out every Saxon faction will unite under one king to fight us, and if that attack fails the Saxons will continue to unite and avenge our hostility.

*'I am damned if I do, and damned if I don't.*

When it came our attack on the monastery at Lindisfarena, one of the holiest sites in Anglo-Saxon Britain, marked the Vikings out as warriors who feared nobody, not even the wrath of God. To Christian Britain, they seemed fearsome and some believed they were sent from hell as a punishment from God. Their more earthly intentions soon became apparent as they stripped the northern cities of gold and precious trinkets, and began to take land to settle. By the time the Great Heathen Army had conquered most of northern and eastern Britain; many despised their conquerors and feared their power, no longer awestruck by their perceived divine origins.

Danelaw has been established in the north and east of Britain as we continue to tear the heart out of the Saxons and their Heptarchy. Northumbria, East Anglia, Essex and large swathes of Mercia must surely fall leaving Wessex and its dependencies to stand alone as the final bastion of Anglo-Saxon Britain. Their situation must be bleak when Alfred and Wessex kingdom is in the swamplands of Sumorsaete.

Monks will be killed in the priory, or thrown into the sea to drown; we may take some young men to be sold as slaves along with their church treasures.

Two of our ships beached in Waymouthe whilst I remained at anchor, but this raid at Lindisfarena will be different; for if we desecrate their site at Holy Island we will have no place to trade, all of Europe will rise up against us.

Let Redwald explain his vision Lord Thorgilssen; for he has foreseen the Anglo-Saxon and Viking age coming to an end in no more than five generations; this will be due to a bastard Lord from Nortmanni called Wilhelm.

# Lindisfarena or Lindisfarne

*"That which has a bad beginning*
*is likely to have a bad ending."*

From Hen-Thorir's Saga

Odin, widely revered as the
king of the gods in Germanic mythology

Ancient map of Holy Island/Lindisfarne
and the Farne Islands

Anglo-Saxon reports of the raid at Lindisfarne

In the year 793 CE, Viking ships attacked the monastery at Lindisfarne on the east coast of England, however a few years earlier three Viking ships were sighted off the coast of Weymouth in Dorset

******

*"On the last day of August, his feast is still observed*
*Aidan, Saint of Lindisfarne, bringer of the word.*
*Bearer of the torch on that Northumbrian shore,*
*Which twice a day and for six hours or more*
*Becomes an island refuge and its rocky core*
*Holds fast the remnants of his cathedral there.*
*And Lindisfarne the singers, a song of theirs"*

## Anglo-Saxon Chronicle (Winchester MS)

*"Here Beorhtric [AD 786-802] took King Offa's daughter Eadburh. And in his days there came for the first time 3 ships; and then the reeve rode there and wanted to compel them to go to the king's town, because he did not know what they were; and they killed him. Those were the first ships of the Danish men which sought out the land of the English race."*

## Such is the entry for AD 789, written by the chronicler a hundred years later.

*"The king's reeve is said to have ridden to the harbour at Portland on the southwest coast of England, thinking the strangers to be traders whom he then would escort to the royal manor at Dorchester. Even though the chronicler identifies the raiders as Danes, the term, like Northmen, was used generically to signify all Scandinavian invaders. The early Vikings tended to be Norwegian, although it was the Danes, who began their pillaging in AD 835, from whom the English suffered the most."*

## A few years later, there is another entry, even more ominous, this time for AD 793.

*"Here terrible portents came about over the land of Northumbria, and miserably frightened the people: these were immense flashes of lightening, and fiery dragons*

*were seen flying in the air. A great famine immediately followed these signs; and a little after that in the same year on 8 June the raiding of heathen men miserably devastated God's church in Lindisfarne Island by looting and slaughter."*

## Anglo-Saxon Chronicle (Petersborough MS)

*"The Viking attack on the holy island of Lindisfarne off the northern coast of Northumbria is the earliest recorded and the best known of the Viking raids in the west. There was situated the monastery of St. Cuthbert, one of the most sacred places of pilgrimage in Britain, and it was there that the Lindisfarne gospels had been copied and illuminated. For more than one hundred and fifty years, Lindisfarne had been a sanctuary of learning and a repository for riches bequeathed by both the pious and the wicked for the repose of their souls. In its chapels and on its altars were golden crucifixes and crosiers, silver pyxes and ciboria, ivory reliquaries, tapestries, and illuminated manuscripts. All were plundered. The attack on Lindisfarne was unprecedented and horrified those who wrote of it.*

*For Alcuin, who was at the court of Charlemagne and a leader of the Carolingian Renaissance, it was inconceivable that ships could suddenly appear from over the horizon. Lo, it is nearly 350 years that we and our fathers have inhabited this most lovely land, and never before has such terror appeared in Britain as we have now suffered from a pagan race, nor was it thought that such an inroad from the sea could be made. Behold, the church of St. Cuthbert spattered with the blood of the priests of God, despoiled of all its ornaments; a place more venerable than all in Britain is given as a prey to pagan peoples."*

## Alcuin, Letter to Ethelred, King of Northumbria

*"So terrible was the attack on God's house that Alcuin sought to justify its occurrence, just as, over two hundred years later, Wulfstan, archbishop of York, would admonish his English brethren for their sins when renewed raids by the Danes had forced Æthelred to flee to Normandy the year before. How else to explain these depredations except that an omnipotent God was deservedly chastising an unworthy people. The calamity of your tribulation saddens me greatly every day, though I am absent; when the pagans desecrated the sanctuaries of God, and poured out the blood of saints around the altar, laid waste the house of our hope, trampled on the bodies of saints in the temple of God, like dung in the street. What assurance is there for the churches of Britain, if St Cuthbert, with so great a number of saints, defends not its own? Either this is the beginning of greater tribulation, or else the sins of the inhabitants have called it upon them. Truly it has not*

*happened by chance, but is a sign that it was well merited by someone. But now, you who are left stand manfully fight bravely, to defend the camp of God."*

## Alcuin, Letter to the Bishop of Lindisfarne another chronicler, working from a lost version of the Anglo-Saxon Chronicle, writes of that fateful year.

*"In that same year the pagans from the northern regions came with a naval force to Britain like stinging hornets and spread on all sides like fearful wolves, robbed, tore and slaughtered not only beasts of burden, sheep and oxen, but even priests and deacons, and companies of monks and nuns. And they came to the church of Lindisfarne, laid everything waste with grievous plundering, trampled the holy places with polluted steps, dug up the altars and seized all the treasures of the holy church. They killed some of the brothers, took some away with them in fetters, many they drove out, naked and loaded with insults, some they drowned in the sea..."*

## Simeon of Durham, Historia Regum in AD 794

*"There was an attack on the Northumbrian monastery at Jarrow, where Bede once had resided, and the year after that, on St. Columba's monastery on the*

*island of Iona. There also were attacks on the coast of Wales and Scotland. In AD 802 and 806, Iona again was devastated. It was as a later entry recorded: the Vikings "burned and demolished, killed abbot and monks and all that they found there, brought it about so that what was earlier very rich was as it were nothing."*

******

## Ragnar's Report

Ragnar Thorgilssen

You will have noticed that every account was written by chroniclers who were not at Lindisfarena that morning, where the fertile land to the south-western section of the island was bereft of humanity.

For if they ever previously witnessed such vulgarity and cruelty that I myself observed they must have been one of the feral cats and dogs we left behind to feed upon the pitiful mutilated bodies of the slaughtered.

I witnessed children no older than ten cheerfully joining the bloodletting, as old and feeble men were grievously slain by the blood stained hands of the foulest of butchers.

The older clerics were disembowelled BEFORE having their throats cut and unceremoniously thrown into the water as naught but surplus waste. The Abbott had his eye's gouged from his sockets, his tongue ripped from his mouth, thereby ensuring he could no longer see or speak the words of Christianity.

Those considered worthwhile to be taken as slaves were castrated prior to them being callously and unsympathetically dragged aboard one of our longboats.

The screams I heard throughout that day will haunt me until my dying days. I personally witnessed old men being hacked to death by inexperienced boys; I found myself unable to watch as his pitiful death throws continued unabated, I had to intervene by showing kindness and mercy by putting the monk out of his misery.

We had landed at Lindisfarena shortly after sunrise when the water was at its highest, the causeway feeding the island was already waterlogged, leaving all cries for help to go unheeded. The spring sunshine had barely touched the land as we approached the priory gathering the monks as we ran forward; those who considered themselves brave tried to prevent the theft of their holy scrolls and books. I later questioned their reasoning - why they sought death to save a few old relics, books and parchments.

Why had they not defended themselves or fought back; incredibly they stood with heads raised and palms held tightly together in the act of prayer as they awaited death.

Taking their gold and trinkets was easy; but that day we committed mass murder of the guiltless on a massive scale, for what I had witnessed rendered me sick to the core. This was never about revenge; what we were doing reminded me of the stories I recalled of ancient Rome and their sickening gladiatorial games. I had seen enough and ran back to my boat; I twisted my head around taking one final glimpse at Lindisfarena. The island had been laid waste by my countrymen, so much unsullied blood had flowed, and for what? We had trampled and smashed their Christian relics; seized their treasure and desecrated their priory alter. I couldn't tell you how many had died that day, but if I said just the one, it would be one too many. I felt nothing but shame and humiliation; how was I to report the events that occurred on that terrible day to my father. I had little doubt if Odin witnessed our heinous crimes against humanity; we would deserve whatever punishment he thought fit.

When I returned home I reported to my father of the numerous atrocities I had witnessed that day, at the same time warning him that the gods would forever take note of our ill-doings on that small island off the coast of north-east Britain.

If I should live long enough to be made Jarl of our land I swore an oath on everything I held sacred that things had to change if trade was to prosper.

Without thinking the words jumped into my mind - *'be strong when you are weak, be brave when you are scared, and be humble when you are victorious.'*

If Odin, in his wisdom, had placed them there - I will never know. From that day onwards to my dying day I would try my utmost to keep to my oath.

# HISTROICAL NOTES

Lindisfarena was the Anglo-Saxon word for Lindisfarena or Holy Island.

Mead is a strong alcoholic drink. All you need to make basic mead is honey, sugar, water and a yeast or bacterial culture; additionally fruit can be added to the mixture.

The quotation - *'most animals after getting drunk would never think about drinking from that same source again, making them much wiser than most men'* originated from Charles Darwin.

Seasickness is a form of motion sickness characterized by a feeling of nausea and, in extreme cases, vertigo, experienced after spending time on a craft on water. Motion sickness is caused by repeated movements when travelling, like going over bumps in a car or moving up and down in a boat. The inner ear sends different signals to the brain from those your eyes are seeing. These confusing messages cause you to feel sick.

Loki is normally portrayed as a scheming coward who cares only for shallow pleasures and self-preservation. He's by turns playful, malicious, a cunning trickster and helpful, but he's always irreverent and nihilistic.

A Jarl was the head of our counsel as well as being an independent Lord in his own right.

The seaux was a short bladed knife or dagger.

Spermaceti is peculiar and much prized oil found in the head of the sperm whale, the actual *"bone"* of the whale which was most commonly used wasn't technically a bone, it was baleen, which was a hard material arrayed in large plates.

The Angles settled in Northumberland and the fen country, known today as East Anglia, whilst the Saxons settled in what today we recognise as Kent, Mercia and Wessex. Over time the Germanic tribes known as the Anglo-Saxon's gradually became just Saxon.

The top edge of the hull of a vessel is called the gunnel, or originally a gunwhale.

From the Bible the Book of Proverbs 28:1 - '*The wicked flee when no one is pursuing, but the righteous are bold as a lion.*'

How the Norsemen saw the trickster 'Loki'

The Mediterranean was originally known as the Middle Sea before being known as the Northern Ocean and then the North Sea, although some older maps depict this as The German Ocean.

In nautical terms the prow of a ship is the forward part of a ship's hull; or the bow.

Hacksilver or hackgold was common among the Norsemen, as a way of paying for goods or wages. Hacksilver may also have been used by Romans in their dealings with Picts.

The Vikings were a seafaring Germanic people from southern Scandinavia who from the late eighth to late eleventh centuries raided, pirated, traded and settled throughout virtually every part of Europe.

The berserkers were savage in battle and their animal-skin attire contributed to the development of the werewolf legend in Europe. The berserker warriors wore bear and wolf skins into battle and normally fought bare-chested on which they painted various Norse symbols.

Feiging as in the phrase - *'Better to be a living feigning than a dead hero,'* means a coward, or one who imitates as in deceiver.

The Vikings explored the nations westward towards England, Iceland, North America, Greenland,

and Vinland as well as to the east and south through Russia to Constantinople, Iran, and Arabia. In the countries they raided and settled, the period is known as the Viking Age, and the term 'Viking' also commonly includes the inhabitants of the Norse homelands. The Vikings had a profound impact on the early medieval history of Scandinavia, the British Isles, France, Estonia, and Kievan Rus'. Kievan Rus' was a loose federation of East Slavic and Finno-Ugric peoples in Europe from the late ninth to the middle of the thirteenth century, under the reign of the Varangian Rurik dynasty.

Colneceastre in Mercia is known today as Colchester.

A snekkja was the smallest of the longship used in warfare and was classified as a ship with at least 20 rowing benches. A typical snekkja might have a length of 17 metres, a beam of 2.5 metres and a draught of only half a metre.

The legend of King Dan giving his name to the Danish people is true, although it is equally true that he did not give his name to the country.

In Norse mythology Aegir was the god of the sea, the Norsemen believed dragons were powerful creatures; they were the embodiment of chaos and destruction.

The mere sight of a dragon foretold the arrival of violent and tumultuous times, which is why dragon heads adorned the bows of the Viking longships that terrorized the coastline of Northern Europe.

The Scandinavian word damned, as in *'to be damned'* roughly translates to *'damnés.'*

The Anglo-Saxon name for Dorset was Dornsaete, or where the Dorn's settled, and the Anglo-Saxon stronghold of Waymouthe was Weymouth; the Kentish town of Dover was known as Dofras, and Hastings was known as Haestingas.

The sea god Aegir

The Scandinavian name for Scotland and the northern isles was Norðreyjar, whereas the Anglo-Saxon's called Scotland Alba.

During the middle ages the market town Malmesbury grew in prominence, it became a centre for learning focused about its Abbey. The future, and first King of all England, King Æthelstan, was laid to rest within the confines of Malmesbury Abbey during the year 939.

The dragon figurehead prominently positioned on the bow of every Viking longboat to signal warlike intentions

Æthelstan was the great grandson of King Alfred. He was never known as Alfred the Great, that title only appeared in books one thousand years after his death.

Odin was both the Lord of Valhalla and the Lord of Asgard. It was there that he gathered his most courageous and fearsome fighters to join him on the field of battle at Ragnarök.

In Norse mythology, Valhalla was a majestic, enormous hall located at Asgard; it was there that Odin ruled over the world. Chosen by Odin, half of those who die in combat travel to Valhalla upon death, led by valkyries, while the other half go to the goddess Freyja's field Fólkvangr. In Valhalla, the dead warriors join the masses of those who have previously died a good death in combat, known as the Einherjar, and various legendary Germanic heroes and kings, as they prepare to aid Odin during the events of Ragnarök.

Freyja was a goddess associated with love, beauty, fertility, sex, war, gold, and seiðr. Freyja is the owner of the necklace Brísingamen, rides a chariot pulled by two cats, is accompanied by the boar Hildisvíni, and possesses a cloak of falcon feathers.

The name Brísingamen can be interpreted in two ways. The second part, "amen" means necklace of torc. The first part, "brísingr" could be a poetic term for fire or amber, suggesting that Brísingamen meant a necklace that gleamed like the sun.

One year's vulgarity is the next year's buzz word, and this is true regarding the Norse words - *'puse or puss'* that is translates to vagina. It is highly probable that both of these words evolved into the modern slang word *'pussy.'*

The Norse Goddess Freya

The Vectis Isle or as the Saxons knew it - Wihtware is more familiarly known as the Isle of Wight. The Romans occupied southern Britain, including the Isle of Wight, for nearly four hundred years, although they never established any townships on the island. It became an agricultural centre; however we know that at least seven Roman villas were built on the Wihtware. The climate, during the time of the Roman occupation was much warmer than today, and it is highly likely that the Romans grew vines there. The *"Men of Wight"* were known as *"Wihtwara"* and the town of Carisbrooke was known as the *"Fort of the Men of Wight"* or *"Wihtwarasburgh"*.

It is possible that the fort may have been named after Wihtgar; but the problem with this theory is that no one knew for certain if Wihtgar existed or was he just another tale. The Anglo-Saxon records show that one of Wihtgar's descendants was alleged to have been Osburh, she being the mother of King Alfred. But can we trust the Anglo-Saxon chronicles to be true? The dilemma with names such as *"Wihtgar"* or *"Wiht"* is that they both had been anglicised from of the Latin word Vecta, which pre-dates the Roman occupation of the Island.

Oxford was known as Oxnaford in Saxon days, its meaning being a ford for oxen, or river crossing for oxen to pass.

Bernica was the Roman name for northern part of Northumberland close to the border with Alba; the names Deira and Bernicia are most probably British in origin, indicating that some British place names retained prevalence after the Anglo-Saxon migrations to Northumbria. Lindisfarena is a small island on the eastern coast of Northumbria. The island can only be reached by small boats, or by means of a man made tidally affected causeway, today Lindisfarena is more commonly known as *"Holy Island."*

The Norse myth regarding the wolf Fenrir is completely true.

The ruins of Lindisfarena Priory

Føkka is a slang Viking word, used as an insult, the English counter is a four letter word beginning with 'f' and ending in 'k'.

Jormungandr, in Norse mythology was a dragon or a snake like creature that lived in the waters surrounding Midgard. Midgard was the visible world of humans. It is said that Odin tossed the creature into the deepest water to keep him from making trouble, however Jormungandr his tail.

Two years prior to the attack at Lindisfane, 'three Norse ships landed off the coast of Weymouth. The administrative officer of the town, known as the reeve, had been ordered by King Ealhmud to detain the strangers and escort them back to the Saxon court, the Vikings, true to their warring nature, took matters into their own hands, and in the ensuing skirmish they killed the king's reeve.

Ériú was the Anglo-Saxon name for Eire, and the translation from Anglo-Saxon to Viking is Dumnionii (Devon). The name for Cornwall was Connibeare, and the name for the River Severn was Afon Hafre.

A Viking rôst equalled a nautical sea mile.

Wales was known as Walentia, and its people were known as Wealh or Saesonin.

Offa's Dyke the barrier between Wales and the Kingdom of Mercia was known as Clawdd Offa

Compulsive evidence of a brutal massacre of Norse warriors has recently been unearthed in Oxnaford. At least thirty-five skeletons were unearthed, all male, aged between sixteen and twenty-five, the wounds endured suggest the all suffered extreme forms of torture prior to death. However, the timeline between the events in this book and those of historical truth do not match; there is a two hundred year disparity between the two events.

Æthelred the Unræd, known to us as Ethelred the unready, ruled the southern Saxon kingdom of Wessex; and by a royal charter ordered the deaths of every Dane in Britain. It was hurriedly drawn up thereby legalising his royal charter.

Æthelred drastic and hasty step was not taken lightly, but was the starting of two hundred years of Anglo-Saxon frustration and nightmare. The Christians preached that the Vikings had long plagued the British Isles with swift raids and conflict; the northern districts of Britain had fallen to the Danes as far south as the city of York. But what was unsettling to the Saxons is that the Norseman had introduced their own form of justice, known as the Danelaw. The men from the north began farming the land and brought their families across the great Northern Ocean forming settlements.

The various Saxon kingdoms were rightfully concerned to see the land being taken from them, but it was not until King Athelstan came to the throne, that the Anglo-Saxons united under one king and became one nation which we know today as - England, the name having its origins from the Anglo-Saxon name for England was Albion, which was originally used when referring to Great Britain, although the origins of this term is not entirely clear, it is claimed the expression meant *"The Kingdom of the Angles."*

Malmesbury during the Anglo-Saxon Viking period was known as Mealdmesbyrig.

Kingston upon Thames was known as Cyninges Tun, meaning simply - the King's estates or the King's town. Its meaning has never been associated as the King's Stone.

Skáli simply means a dwelling place.

The phrase 'Good riddance etc.' is taken from the following John Rastell's poem, *"Away Mourning"*, and c1525

*I haue her lost,*
*For all my cost,*
*Yet for all that I trowe*
*I haue perchaunce,*

*A fayre ryddaunce,*
*And am quyt of a shrew.*

Berserkers were said to have fought with a trance-like fury, most probably caused through taking a drugged plant or mushroom, a characteristic which later gave rise to the modern English word *'berserk or beserker.'*

The Berserkers were physically powerful warriors with an ursine aspect. These hideous creatures, dressed in wolf or bear skins, were the first to enter the field of battle, highly drugged, and the last to retire; the Berserkers believed that there was not a weapon or fire could harm them. The word 'Berserker' evolved from 'bear-shirt,' however others suggest the word 'bear' was originally 'bare' as in being bare-chested.

The Berserjker

In Saxon times the town of Jarrow was known as Donaemuth and the county of Kent was known as Cent.

King Egbert otherwise known as Ecgberht, reined in Wessex between 802 and 839 when he was succeeded by his son Æthelwulf, who was King of Wessex between 839 and 858. In the year 825, Egbert, defeated King Beornwulf of Mercia, which ended a prolonged Mercian dominance over Anglo-Saxon Britain south of the Humber? The Holy Island of Lindisfarena, commonly known as either Holy Island or Lindisfarena, is a tidal island off the northeast coast of England. Holy Island has a recorded history reaching as far back as the sixth century; it was an important centre of Celtic

Christianity under Saints Aidan of Lindisfarena, Cuthbert, Eadfrith of Lindisfarena and Eadberht of Lindisfarena.

By the time the Great Heathen Army had conquered northern and eastern England in the 870s, many in England despised their conquerors and feared their power, no longer awestruck by the perceived divine origins.

After the Danish invasion and the Norman Conquest a priory was eventually re-established on Holy Island.

The chronicles written of the attack at Lindisfarena describe the following -

*Here were dreadful forewarnings come over the land of Northumbria, and woefully terrified the people: these were amazing sheets of lightning and whirlwinds, and fiery dragons were seen flying in the sky. A great famine soon followed these signs, and shortly after in the same year, on the sixth day before the ides of June, the woeful inroads of heathen men destroyed God's church in Lindisfarena Island by fierce robbery and slaughter.*

The Anglo-Saxon Chronicle indicated the raid took place in the month of January, however, it is now generally accepted that the actual date must have taken place in June. The testimony quoted from other sources show spring as a more favourable season for coastal raiding.

The given date probably represents a scribal error.

The English counties Norðfolc and Elklet are known today as Norfolk and Suffolk (the later meaning the southern folk of the East Angles, probably named after the Lady Elflet or Alflet whose name is mentioned in the Domesday Book).

The month of Eastre is known today as April, although its roots come from the Christian festival of Easter. Additionally the month known to the Vikings as Skerpla is June. The Vikings did not have four seasons as we do today; they only had two seasons, summer and winter. Their year was not divided into months as most countries do today. The moon was very important to the Vikings to keep track of time it was the sun that had the central role in Viking culture. Due to the fact that Denmark had long seasons of cold and dark, the sun was not only the bringer of light but also life. It is when the sun is high in the sky that it was possible to work the land plant and harvest the crops.

Hnefatafl was a Viking board game, similar to chess.

Nortmanni or Normandy takes its name from the Viking invaders who menaced large parts of Europe towards the end of the first millennium. Its meaning is *"Men from the North".*

Redwald's vision as shown, although true in context; Redwald is an imaginary character, although I have no doubt it was probably a reasonably common name in the period.

Somerset in Saxon times was known as Sumorsaete

National Flag of Denmark
A red background with a white cross

## Redwald's vision

In the early years of the eleventh century, three battles contributed to the end of the Anglo-Saxon and Viking era for once for all, and heralded the introduction of the Norman dynasty to England's shores.

The first skirmish was at Fulford Gate, a small village on the outskirts of York, when on the twentieth day of September 1066 a hastily assembled English army commanded by two Northern Earls, Edwin and Morcar, fought against an alliance of Vikings lead by King Harald Hardrada and King Harold's banished brother Tostig Godwinson. The battle began with the English force spreading out to secure their flanks. On their right flank was the River Ouse, and on the left was the swampy region known as Fordland. The northern Earls struck first, advancing on the Danes before they could fully deploy. Morcar's troops pushed the Danish force back into the marshlands; however the Anglo-Saxon army were forced to give ground. Edwin's soldiers who had defended the bank were now cut off from Morcar's force by the marshland, where they were heavily defeated. King Harold Godwinson was forced to march his army from his London base to York, a distance of one hundred and ninety miles; five days later Harold surprised the Danes at Stamford Bridge where King Harald Hardrada and Tostig Godwinson's were killed and their combined armies routed.

Harold, the last Anglo-Saxon King of England, hearing that Wilhelm the bastard Duke Normanni had successfully landed his troops at Pevensey Bay, was again forced to march back south where the two armies struggled throughout the day; eventually Harold was killed and his army utterly destroyed.

Lest we forget those brave Englishmen who gave their lives for their country on that fearsome day on the fourteenth day of October 1066 on a green field turned red with the blood of the dead, eight miles northwest of Hastings; that village was thereafter known as "Battle"

*Beware of an old man in a profession where men usually die young!*

Jarl Tor Thorgilssen

The 325-line fragment ends with the rallying speech of the old warrior Byrhtwold (here in modern English):

*"Mind must be firmer, heart the more fierce,
Courage the greater, as our strength diminishes."*

Printed in Great Britain
by Amazon